# THE SCHOOL MUSICAL MELTDOWN

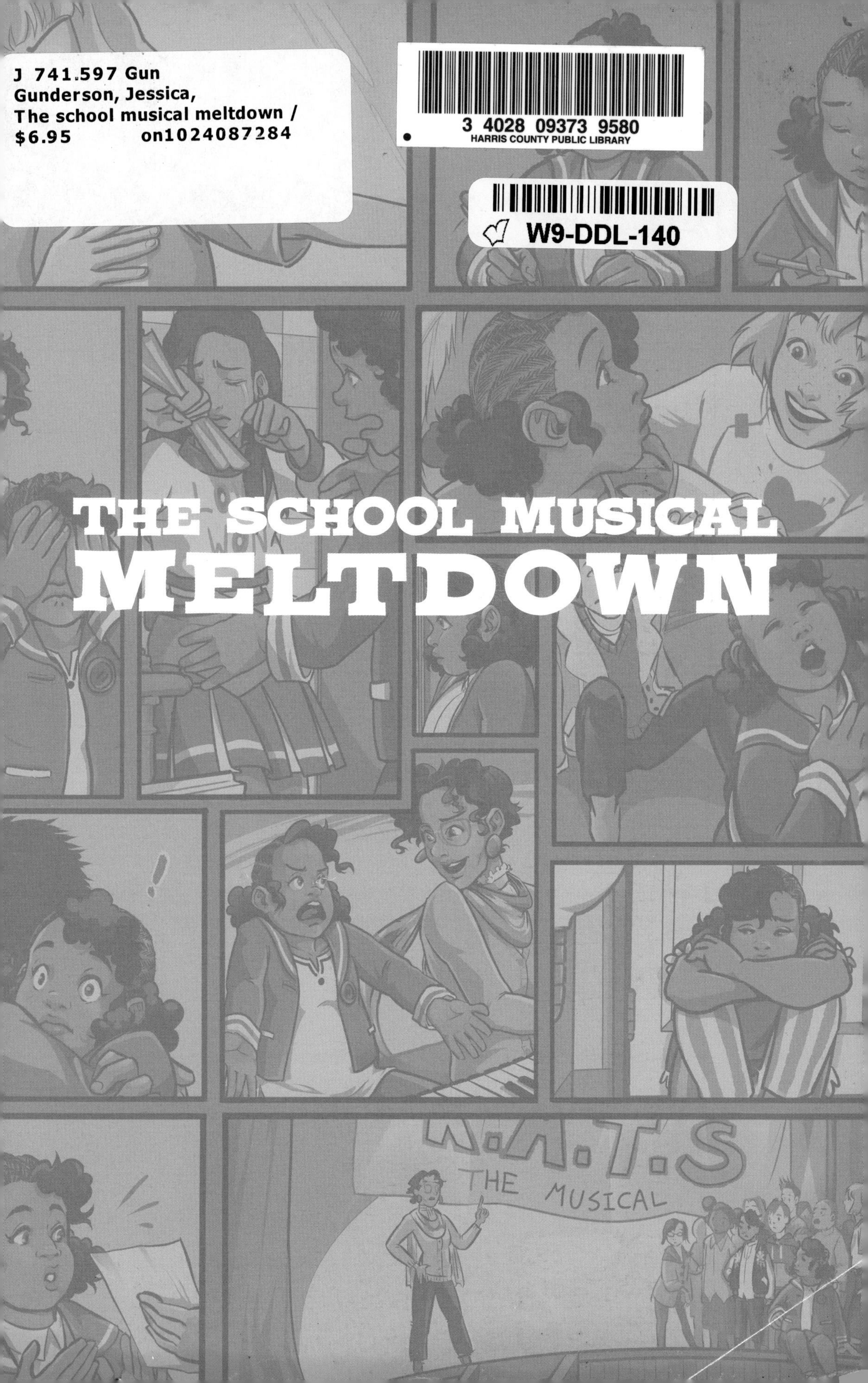
!
THE MUSICAL

JUNIOR HIGH DRAMA IS PUBLISHED BY
STONE ARCH BOOKS
A CAPSTONE IMPRINT
1710 ROE CREST DRIVE
NORTH MANKATO, MINNESOTA 56003
WWW.MYCAPSTONE.COM

Summary: Kamilla is an amazing singer, but she refuses to try out for the school musical. She simply can't stand the thought of everyone staring at her, when she sees herself as overweight. Led by her mom, Kamilla sees a doctor who tells her she's a healthy weight but encourages her to exercise to feel better, both physically and mentally. Will Kamilla's new habit lead to big changes, or is she stuck waiting in the wings forever?

CATALOGING-IN-PUBLICATION DATA IS AVAILABLE ON THE LIBRARY OF CONGRESS WEBSITE.
ISBN: 978-1-4965-4711-8 (LIBRARY BINDING)
ISBN: 978-1-4965-7414-5 (PAPERBACK)
ISBN: 978-1-4965-4716-3 (EBOOK PDF)

EDITOR: JULIE GASSMAN
DESIGNER: ASHLEE SUKER
CREATIVE DIRECTOR: NATHAN GASSMAN

Printed in the United States of America.
PA017

Excerpts from OLD POSSUM'S BOOK OF CATS by T.S. Eliot. Copyright © 1939 by T.S. Eliot, renewed 1977 by Esme Valerie Eliot. Reprinted by permission of Houghton Mifflin Harcourt Publishing Company. All rights reserved.
Extract taken from MEMORY, Copyright Andrew Lloyd Webber, Tim Rice and T.S. Eliot, first appeared in OLD POSSUM'S BOOK OF CATS. Reproduced by permission of Faber & Faber Ltd.

# JUNIOR HIGH DRAMA

## THE SCHOOL MUSICAL
# MELTDOWN

by Jessica Gunderson

illustrated by Sumin Cho

STONE ARCH BOOKS
a capstone imprint

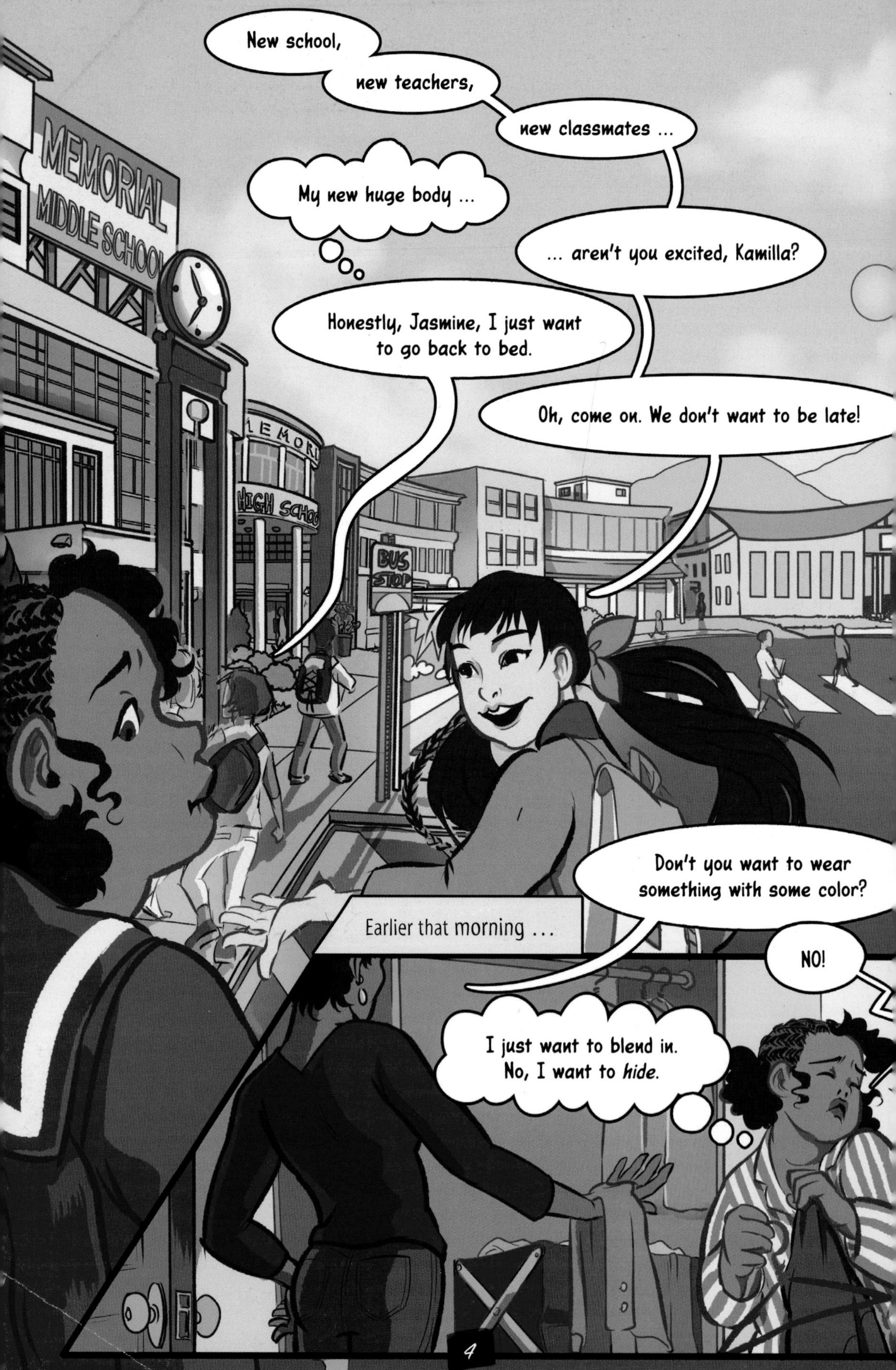
MEMORIAL MIDDLE SCHOOL
New school,
new teachers,
new classmates ...
My new huge body ...
... aren't you excited, Kamilla?
Honestly, Jasmine, I just want to go back to bed.
Oh, come on. We don't want to be late!
MEMORIAL HIGH SCHOOL
BUS STOP
Don't you want to wear something with some color?
Earlier that morning ...
NO!
I just want to blend in. No, I want to *hide*.

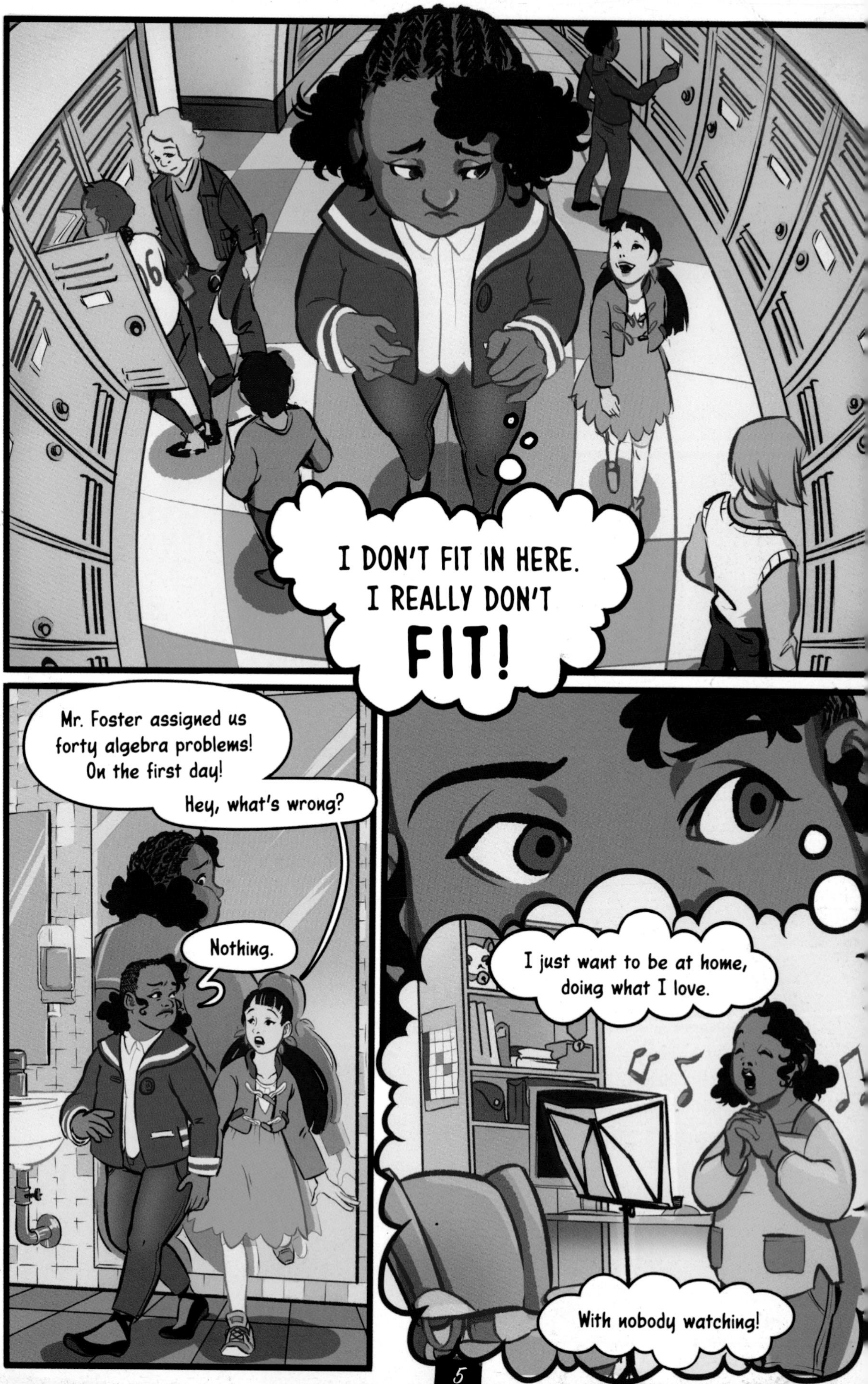
I DON'T FIT IN HERE. I REALLY DON'T FIT!
Mr. Foster assigned us forty algebra problems! On the first day!
Hey, what's wrong?
Nothing.
I just want to be at home, doing what I love.
With nobody watching!

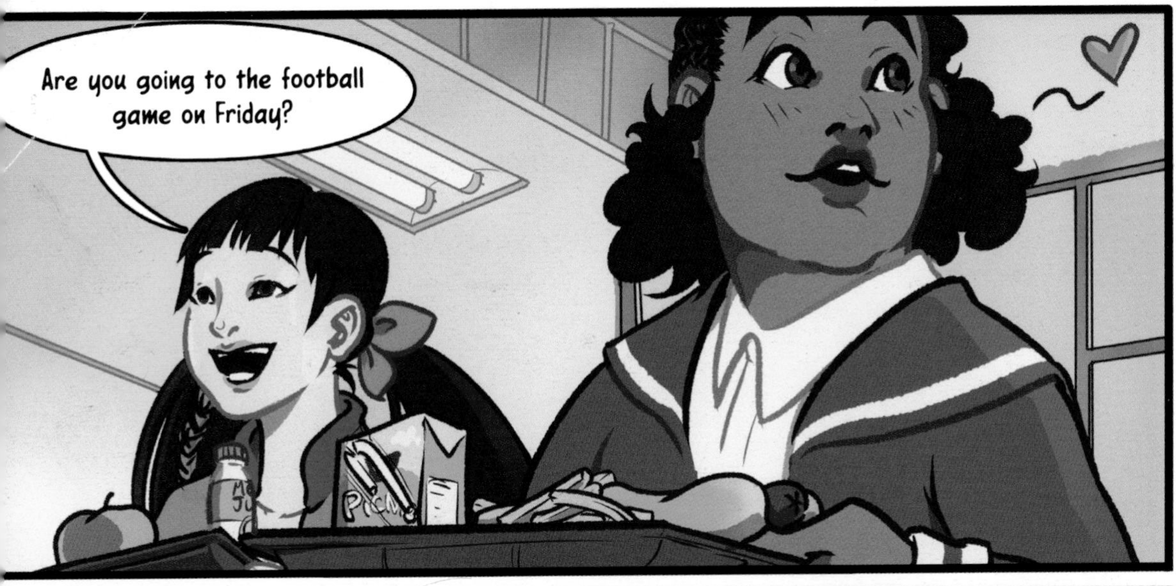
Are you going to the football game on Friday?

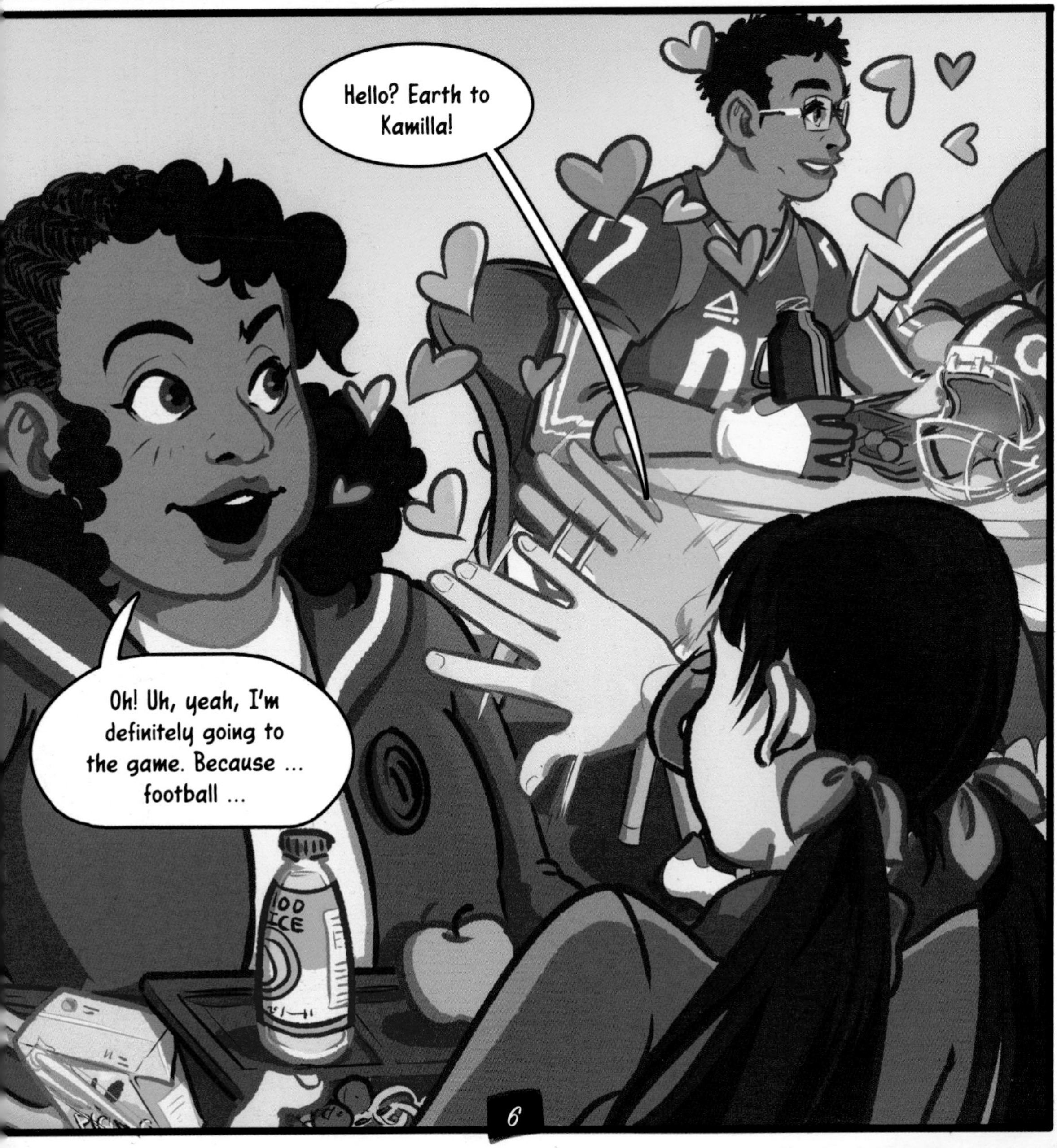
Hello? Earth to Kamilla!
Oh! Uh, yeah, I'm definitely going to the game. Because ... football ...

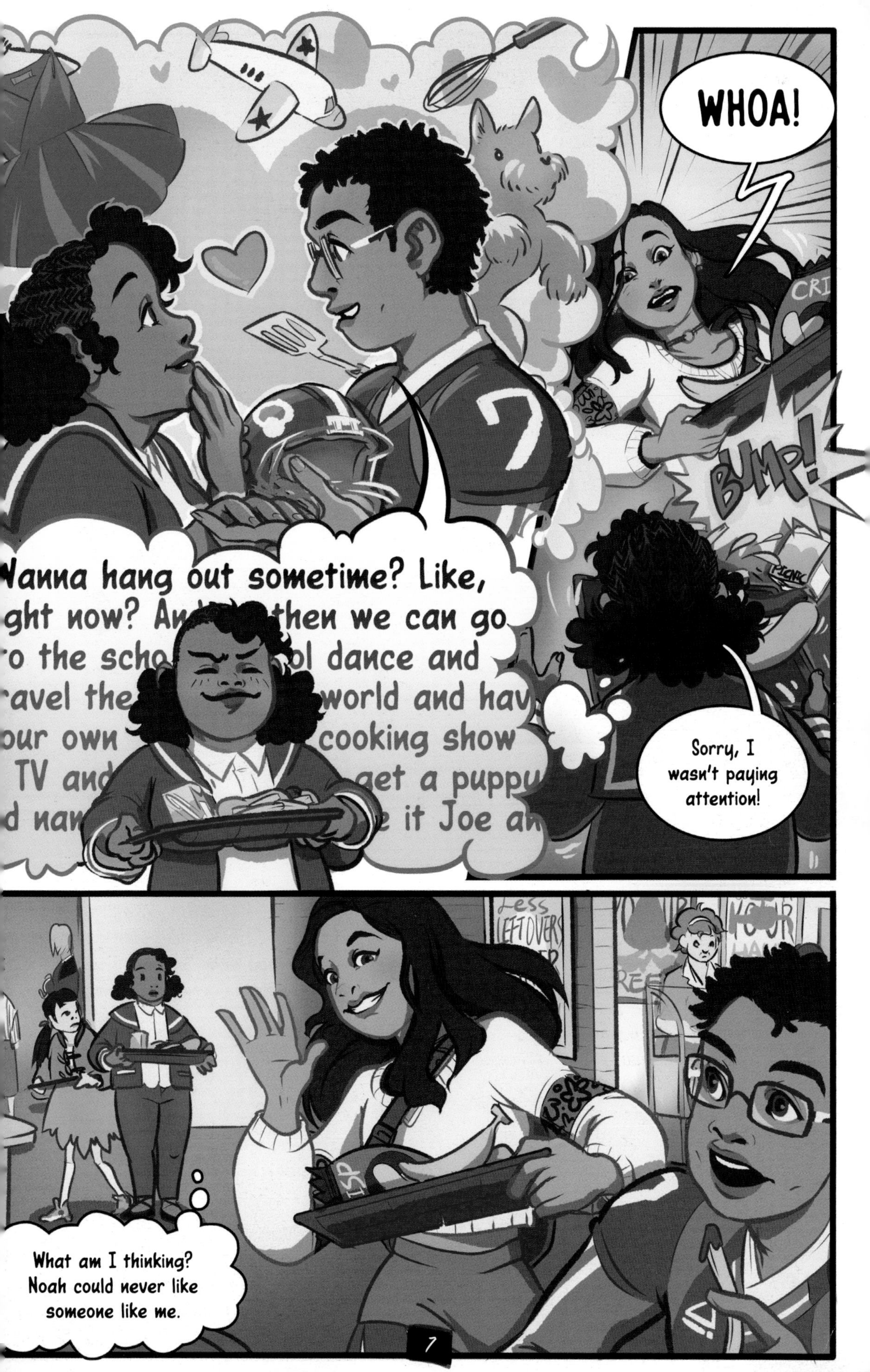
WHOA!
BUMP!
Vanna hang out sometime? Like,
ght now? An then we can go
o the scho ol dance and
avel the world and hav
our own cooking show
TV and get a puppy
d nam e it Joe an
Sorry, I wasn't paying attention!
Less LEFTOVERS
What am I thinking? Noah could never like someone like me.

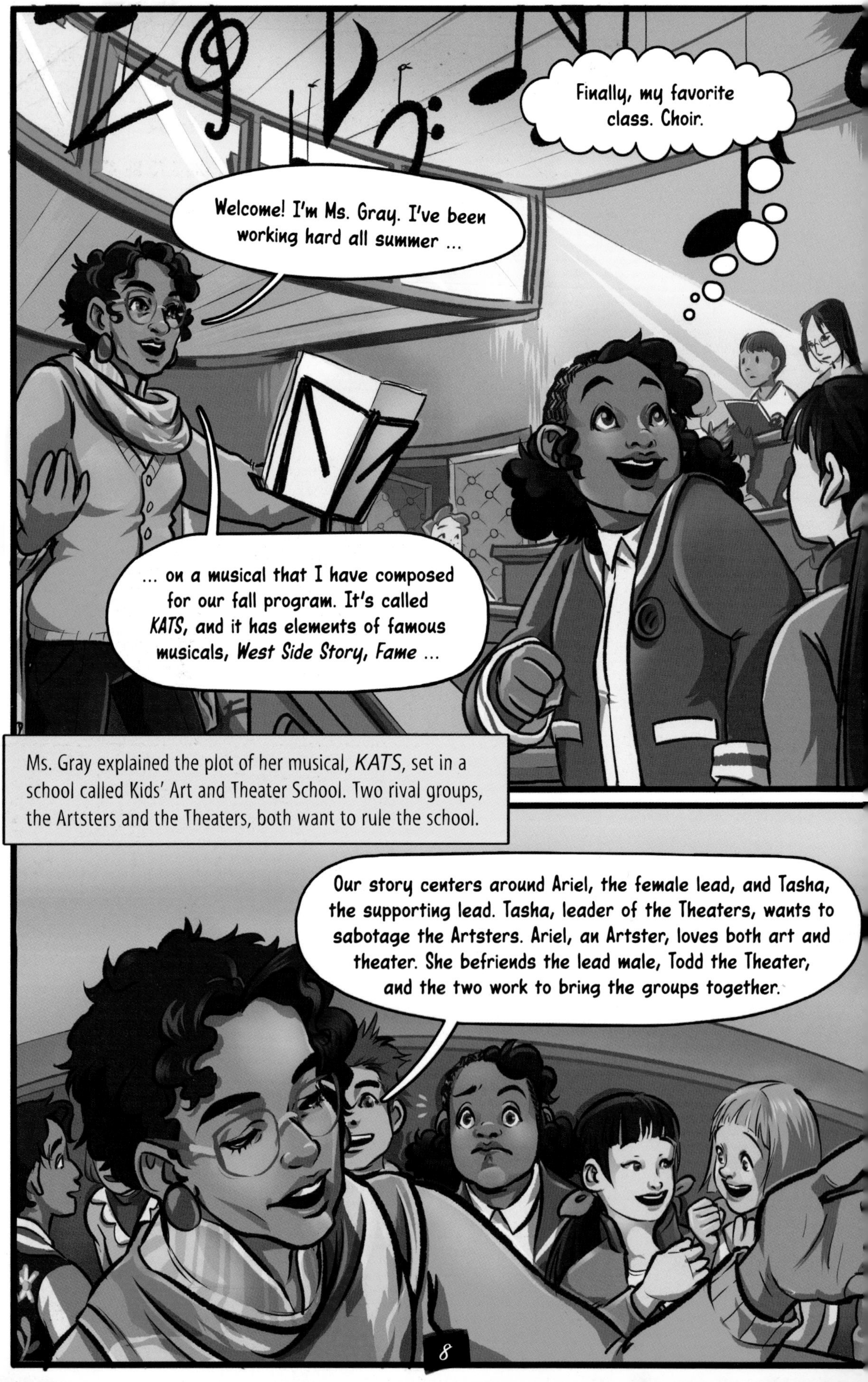
Finally, my favorite class. Choir.
Welcome! I'm Ms. Gray. I've been working hard all summer ...
... on a musical that I have composed for our fall program. It's called *KATS*, and it has elements of famous musicals, *West Side Story*, *Fame* ...
Ms. Gray explained the plot of her musical, *KATS*, set in a school called Kids' Art and Theater School. Two rival groups, the Artsters and the Theaters, both want to rule the school.
Our story centers around Ariel, the female lead, and Tasha, the supporting lead. Tasha, leader of the Theaters, wants to sabotage the Artsters. Ariel, an Artster, loves both art and theater. She befriends the lead male, Todd the Theater, and the two work to bring the groups together.

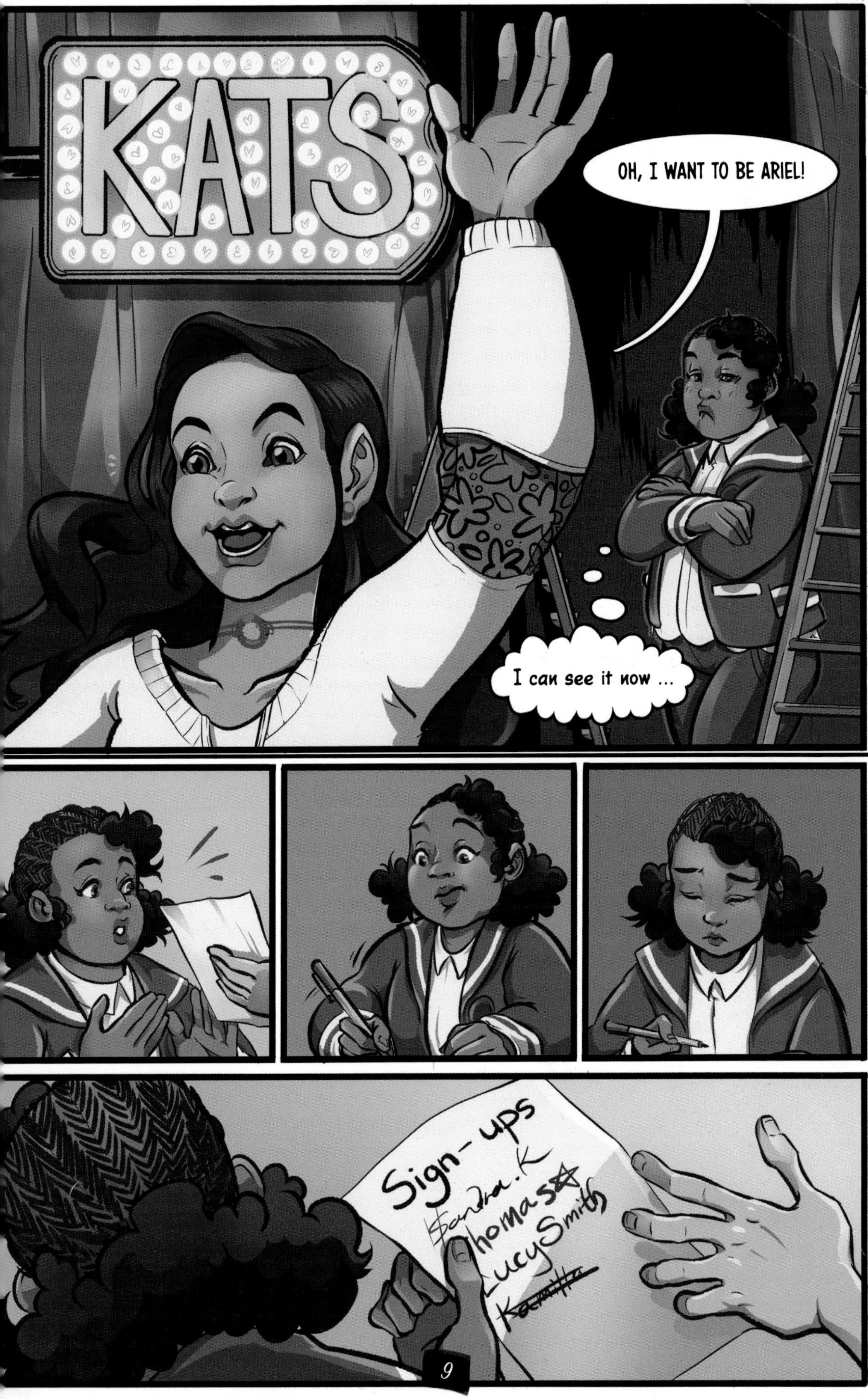
KATS
OH, I WANT TO BE ARIEL!
I can see it now ...
Sign-ups
Sandra.K
Thomas
LucySmith

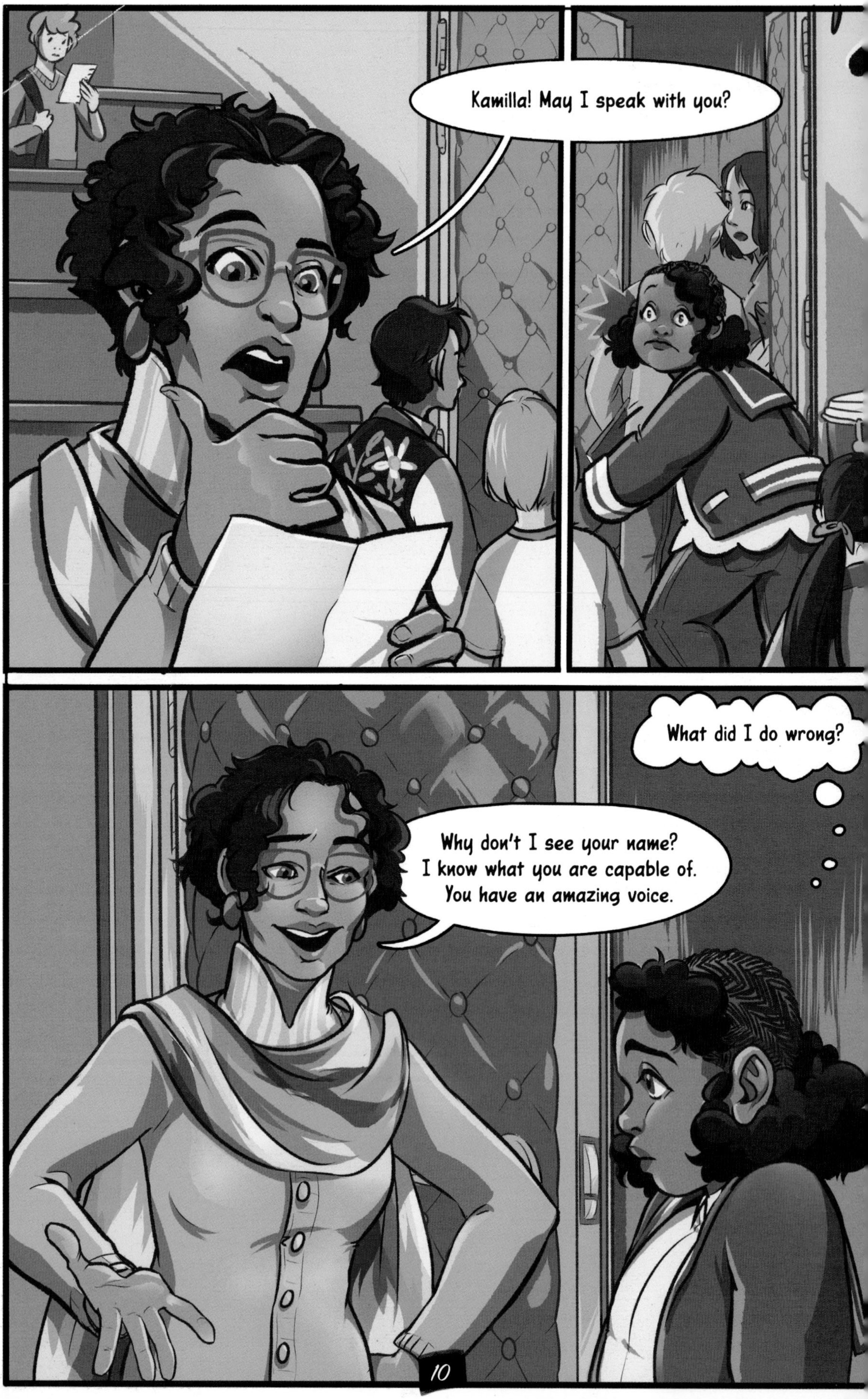
Kamilla! May I speak with you?
What did I do wrong?
Why don't I see your name? I know what you are capable of. You have an amazing voice.

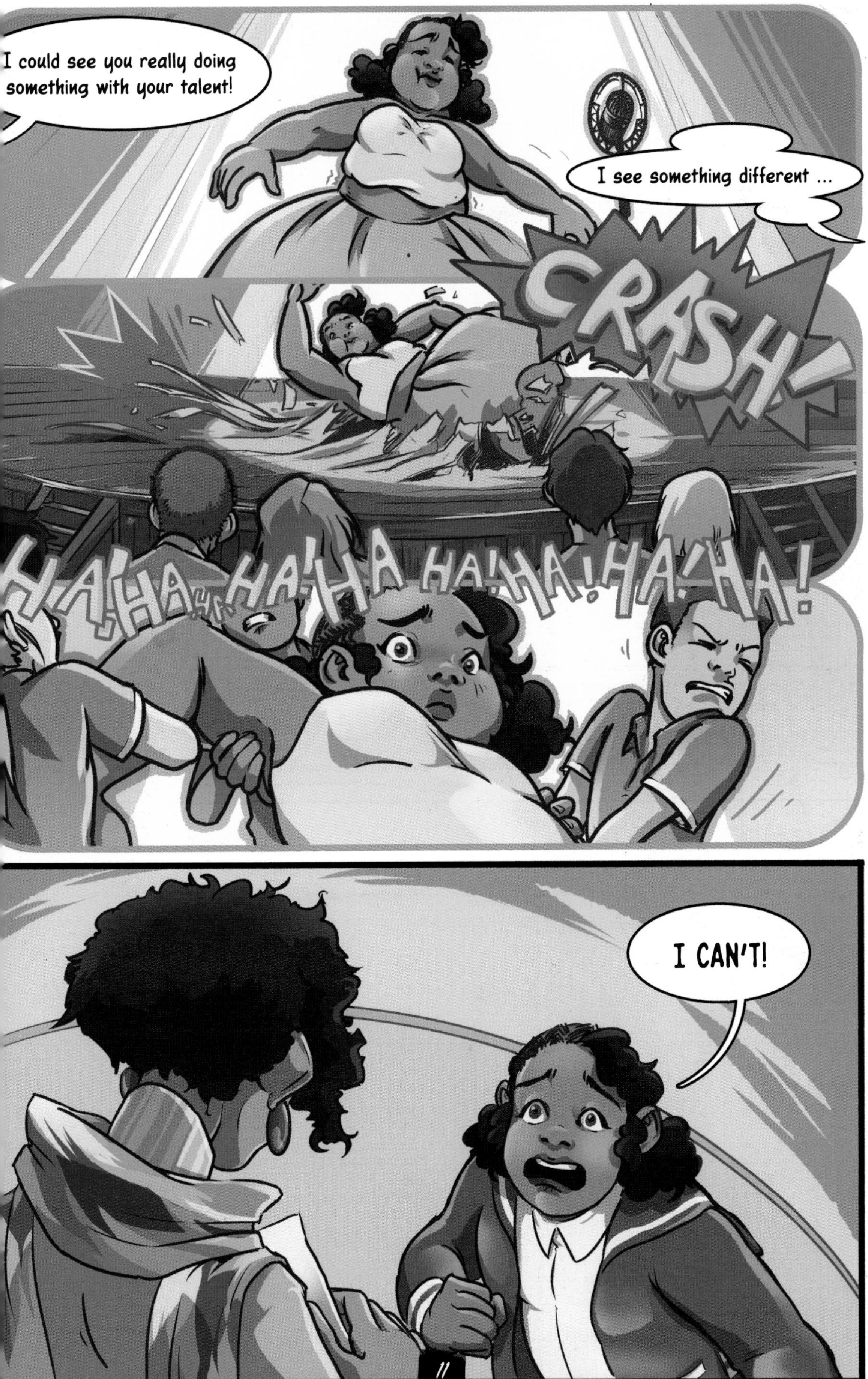
I could see you really doing something with your talent!
I see something different ...
CRASH!
HA! HA! HA! HA! HA! HA! HA! HA! HA!
I CAN'T!

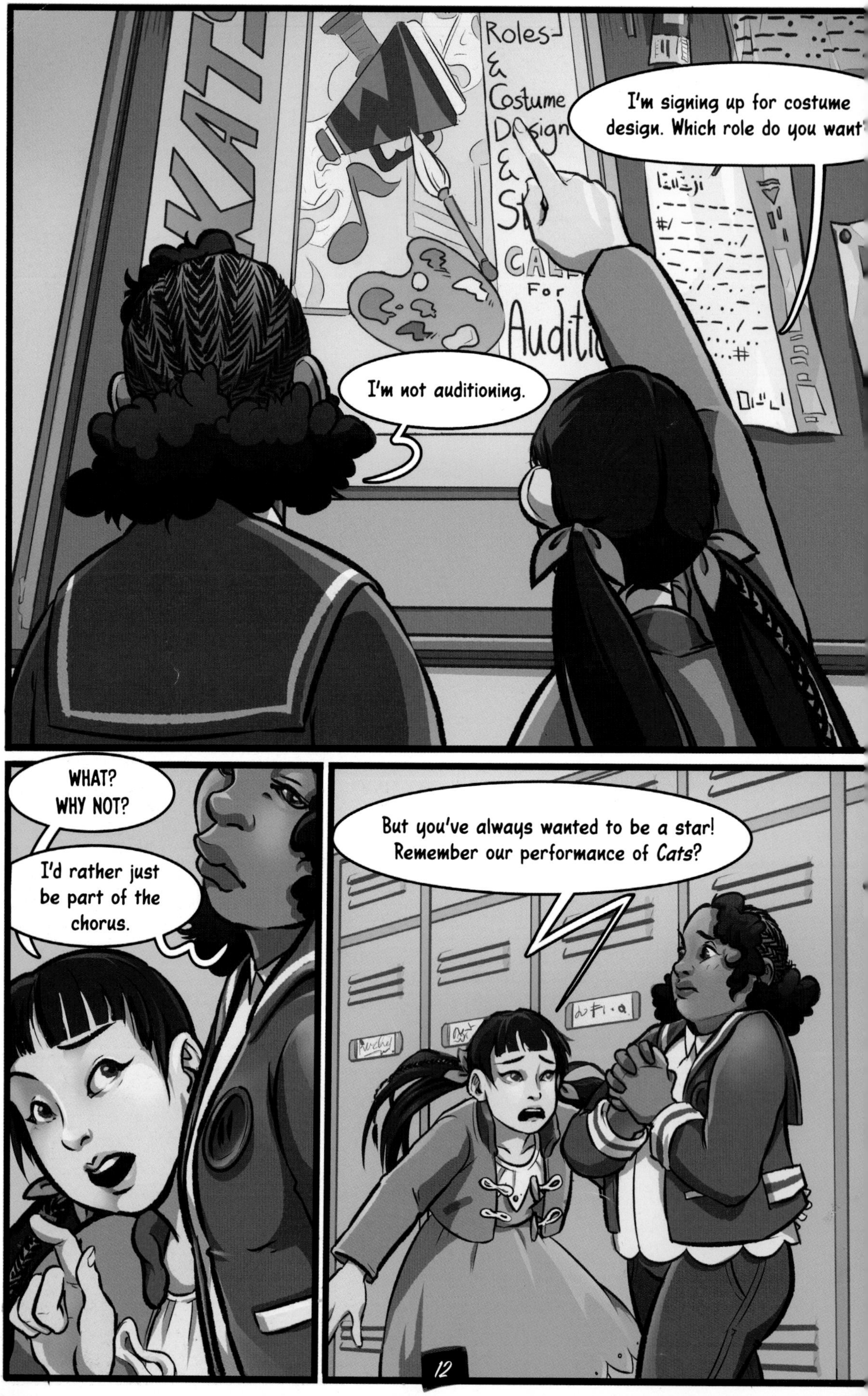
I'm signing up for costume design. Which role do you want?
I'm not auditioning.
WHAT? WHY NOT?
I'd rather just be part of the chorus.
But you've always wanted to be a star! Remember our performance of *Cats*?

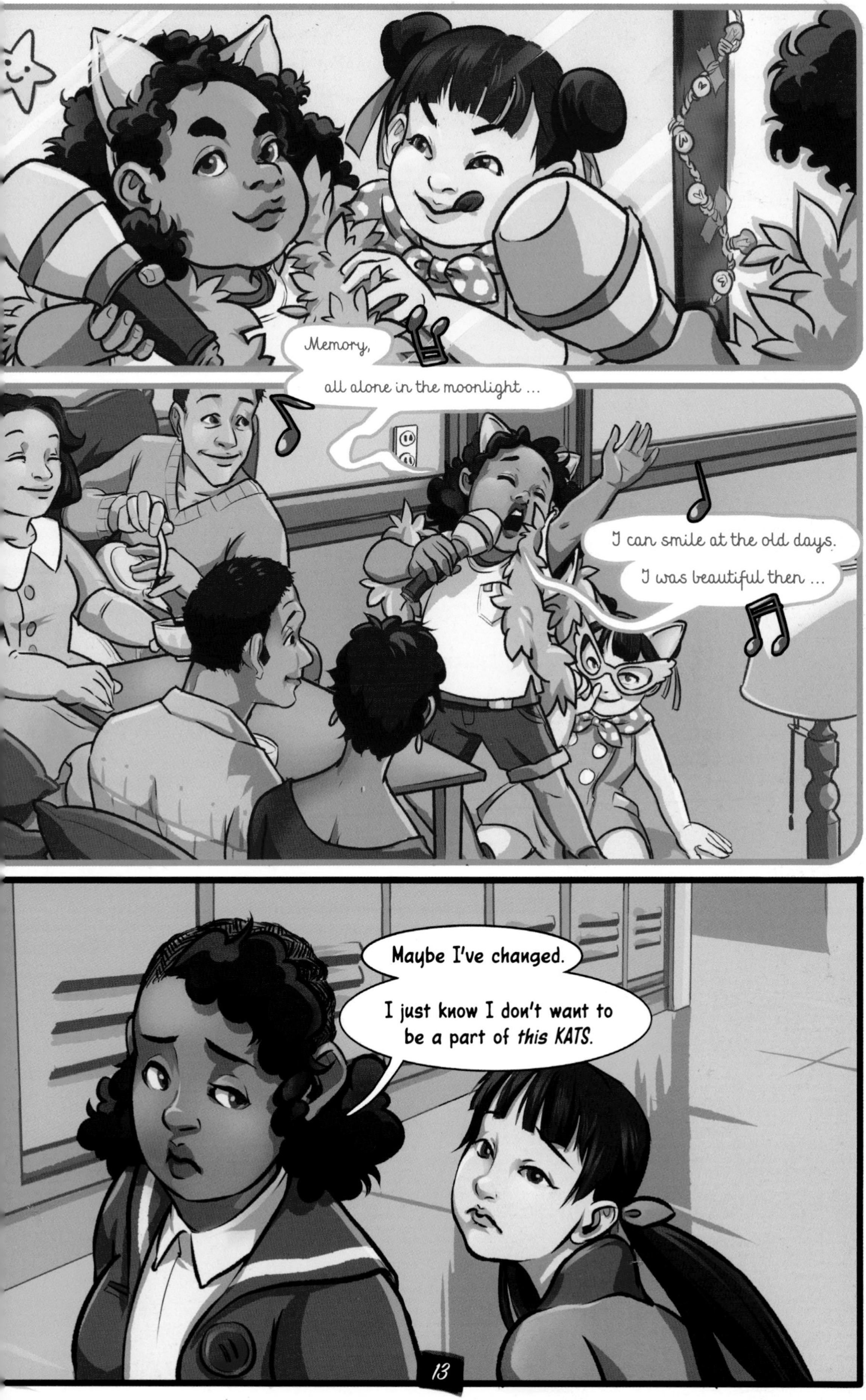
Memory,
all alone in the moonlight ...
I can smile at the old days.
I was beautiful then ...
Maybe I've changed.
I just know I don't want to be a part of *this KATS*.

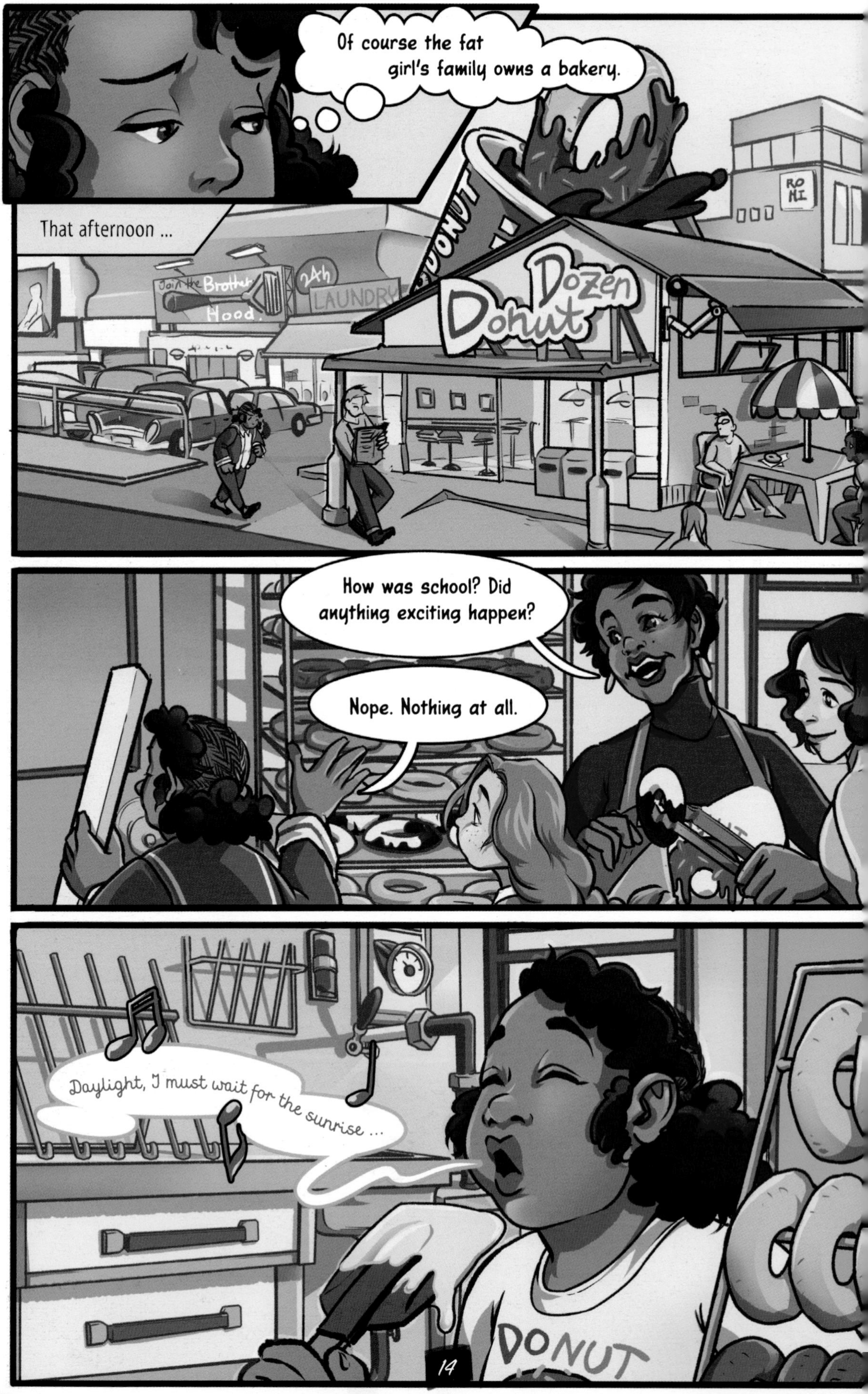
Of course the fat girl's family owns a bakery.
That afternoon ...
DONUT
Dozen Donut
24h LAUNDRY
How was school? Did anything exciting happen?
Nope. Nothing at all.
Daylight, I must wait for the sunrise ...
DONUT

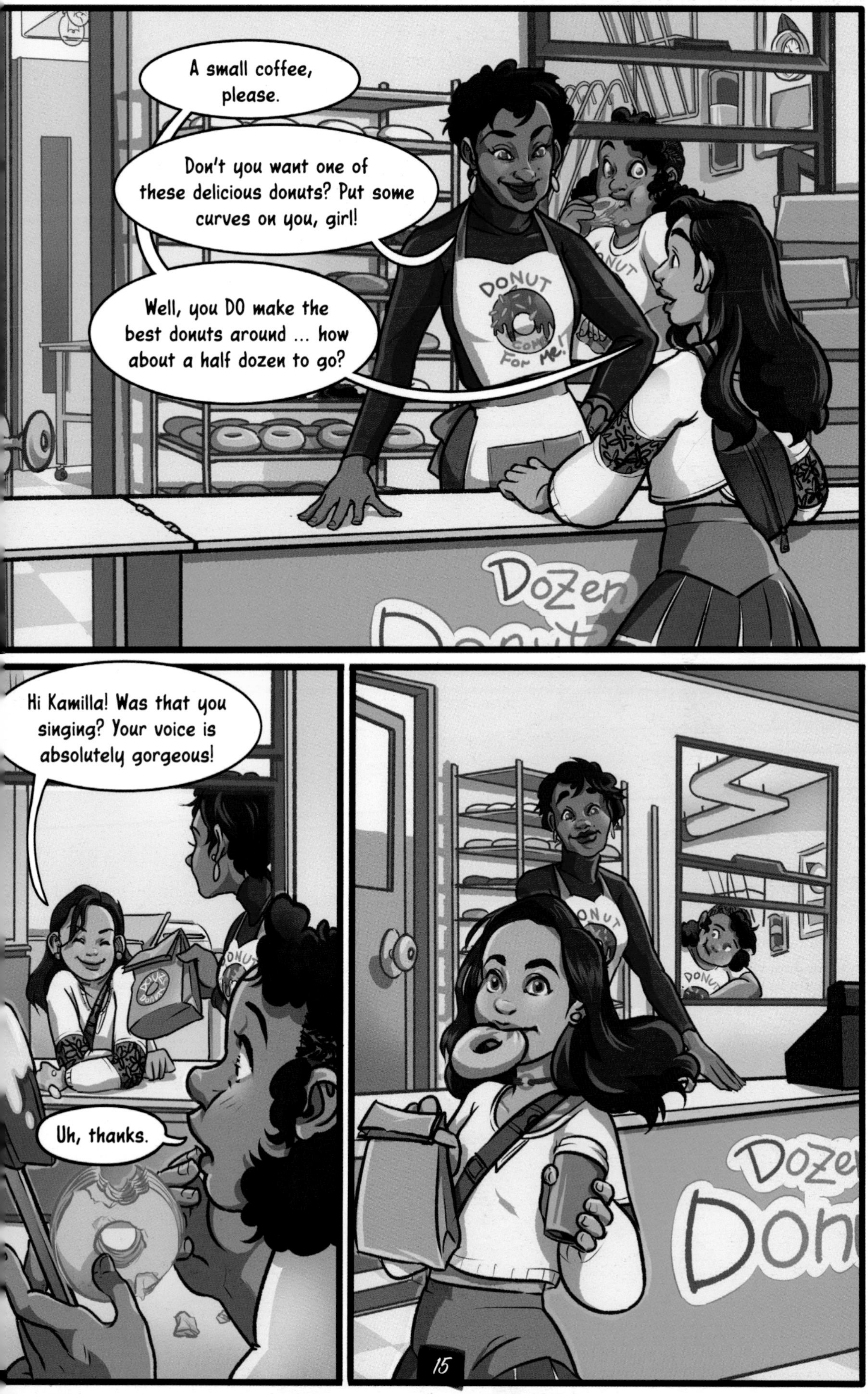
A small coffee, please.
Don't you want one of these delicious donuts? Put some curves on you, girl!
Well, you DO make the best donuts around ... how about a half dozen to go?
DONUT COME FOR ME!
Dozen
Hi Kamilla! Was that you singing? Your voice is absolutely gorgeous!
Uh, thanks.
Dozen Don

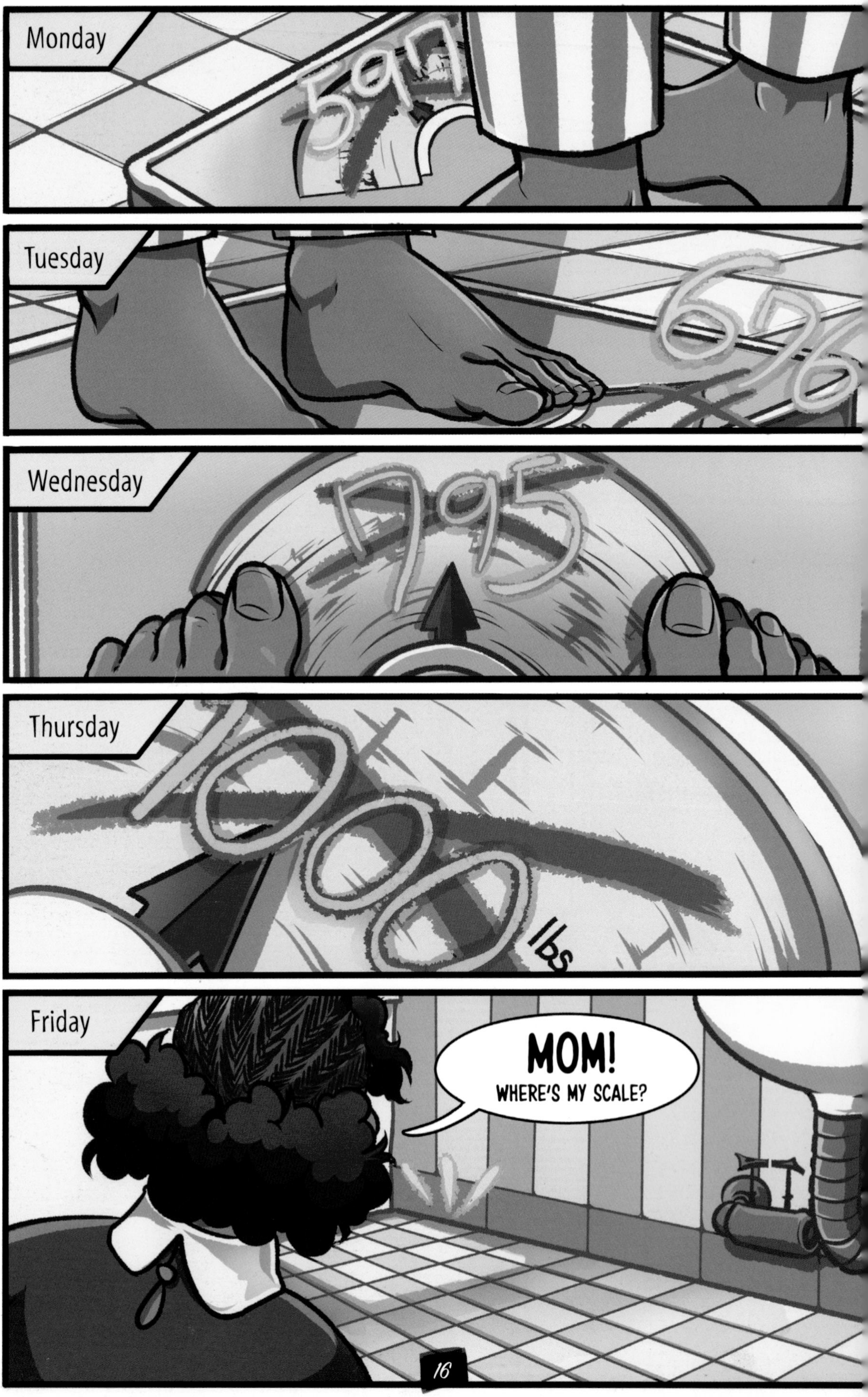
Monday
597
Tuesday
696
Wednesday
795
Thursday
1000
lbs
Friday
MOM!
WHERE'S MY SCALE?

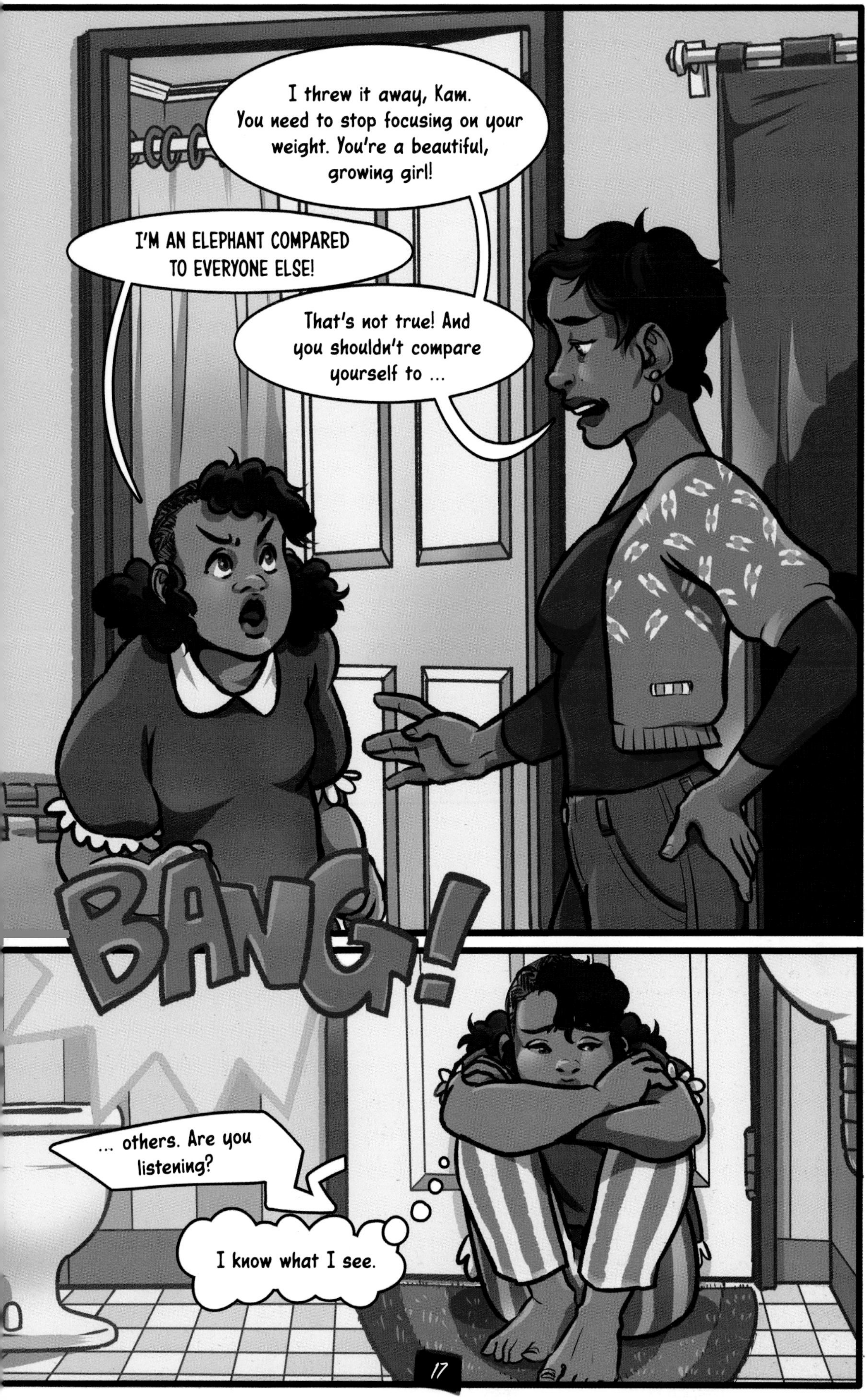
I threw it away, Kam. You need to stop focusing on your weight. You're a beautiful, growing girl!
I'M AN ELEPHANT COMPARED TO EVERYONE ELSE!
That's not true! And you shouldn't compare yourself to ...
BANG!
... others. Are you listening?
I know what I see.

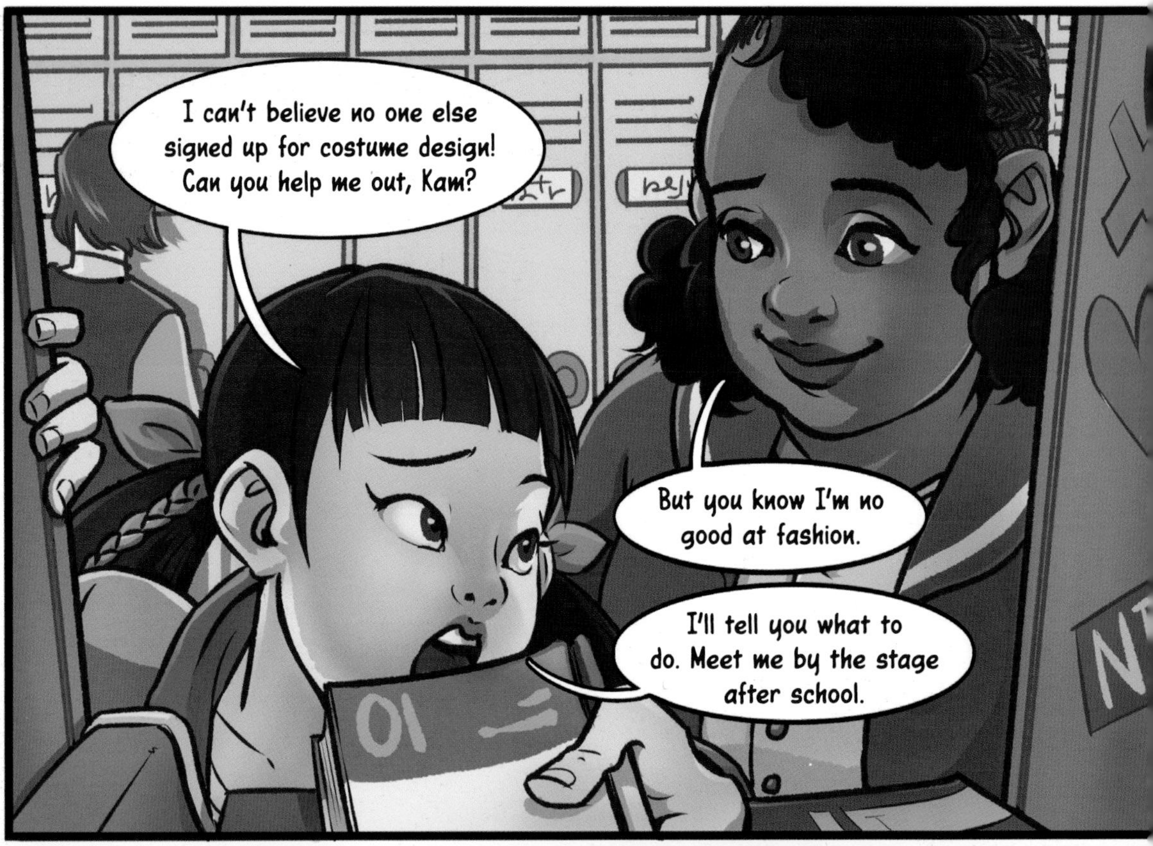
I can't believe no one else signed up for costume design! Can you help me out, Kam?
But you know I'm no good at fashion.
I'll tell you what to do. Meet me by the stage after school.

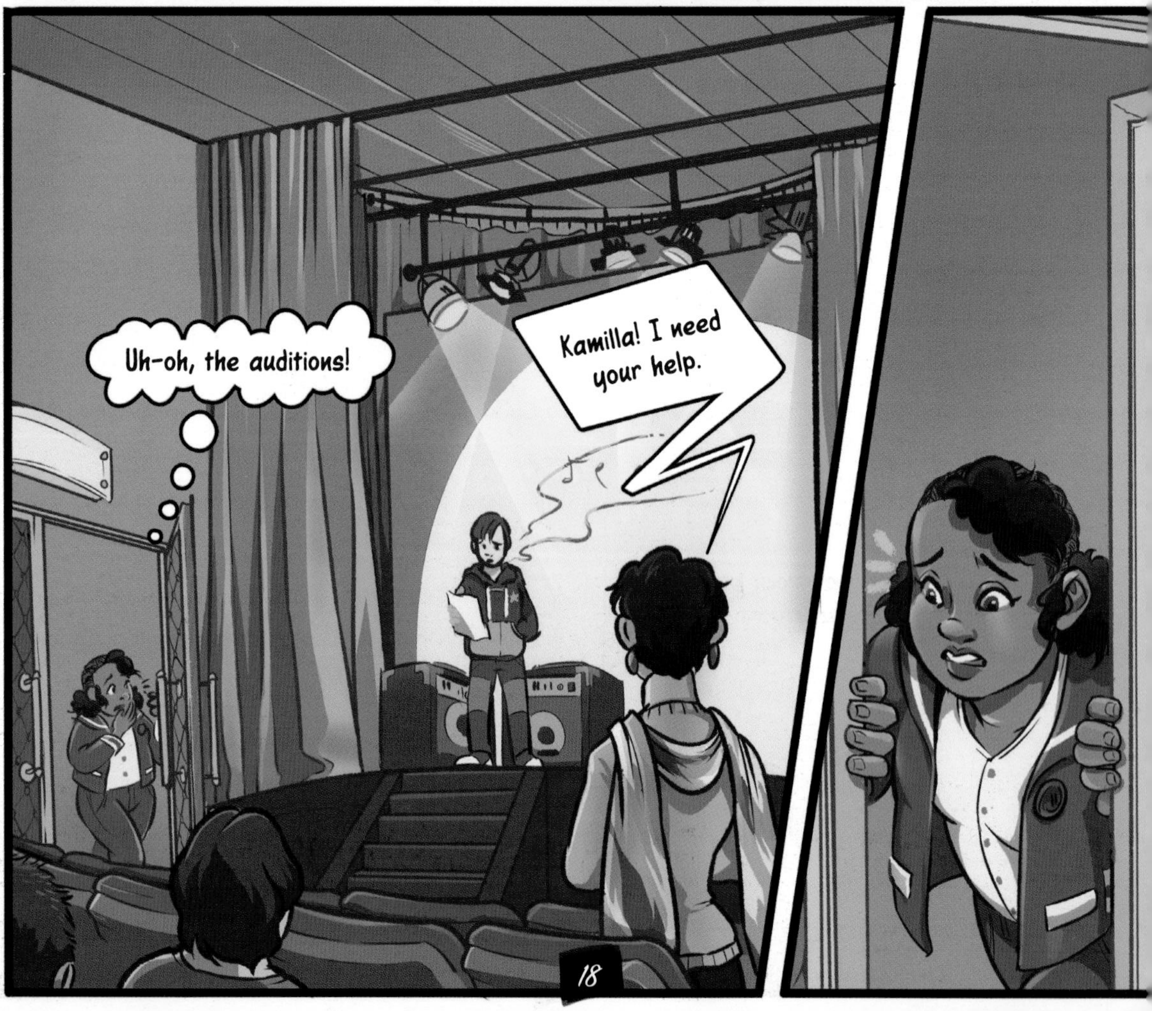
Uh-oh, the auditions!
Kamilla! I need your help.

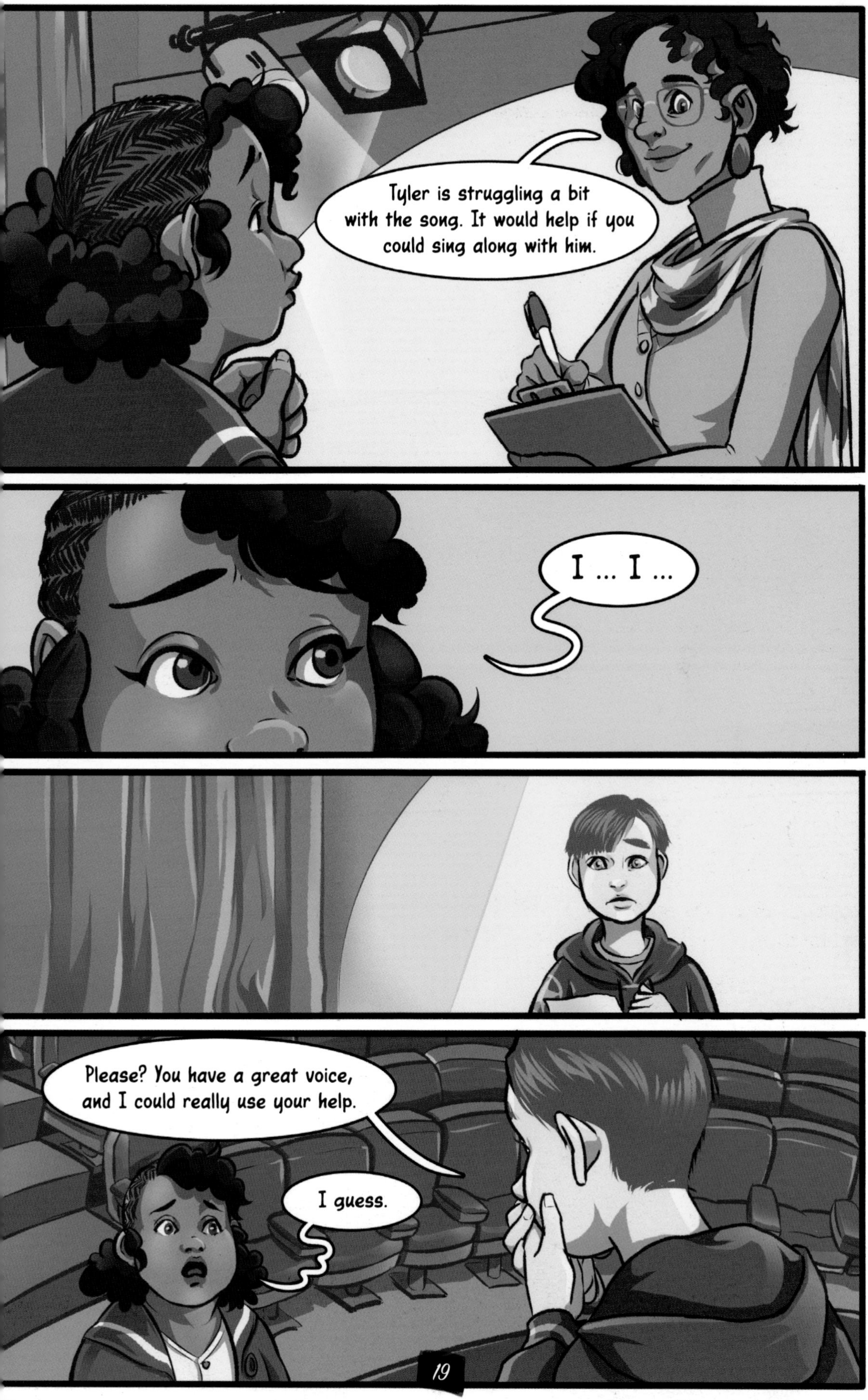
Tyler is struggling a bit with the song. It would help if you could sing along with him.
I ... I ...
Please? You have a great voice, and I could really use your help.
I guess.

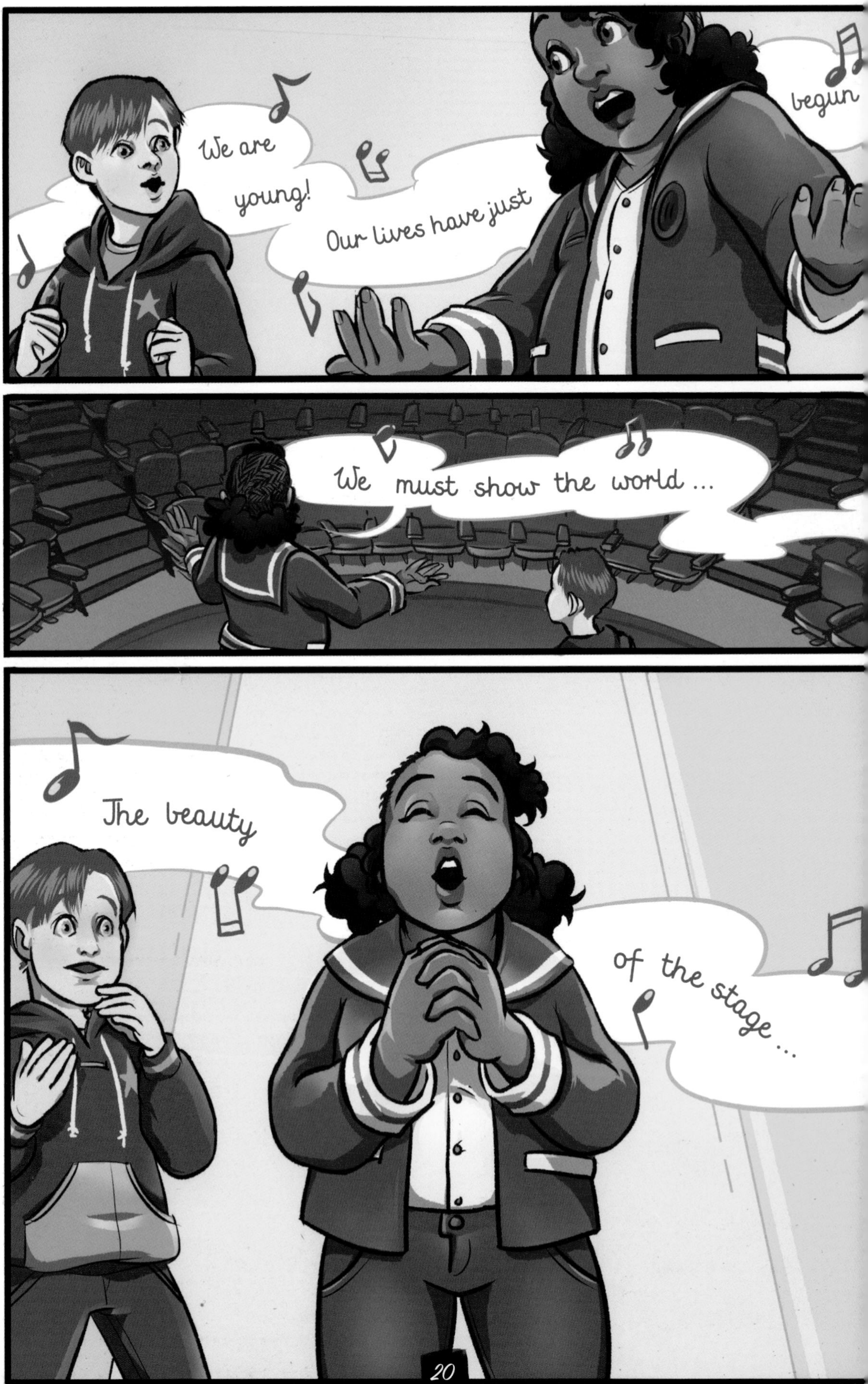
We are young!
Our lives have just
begun
We must show the world ...
The beauty
of the stage ...

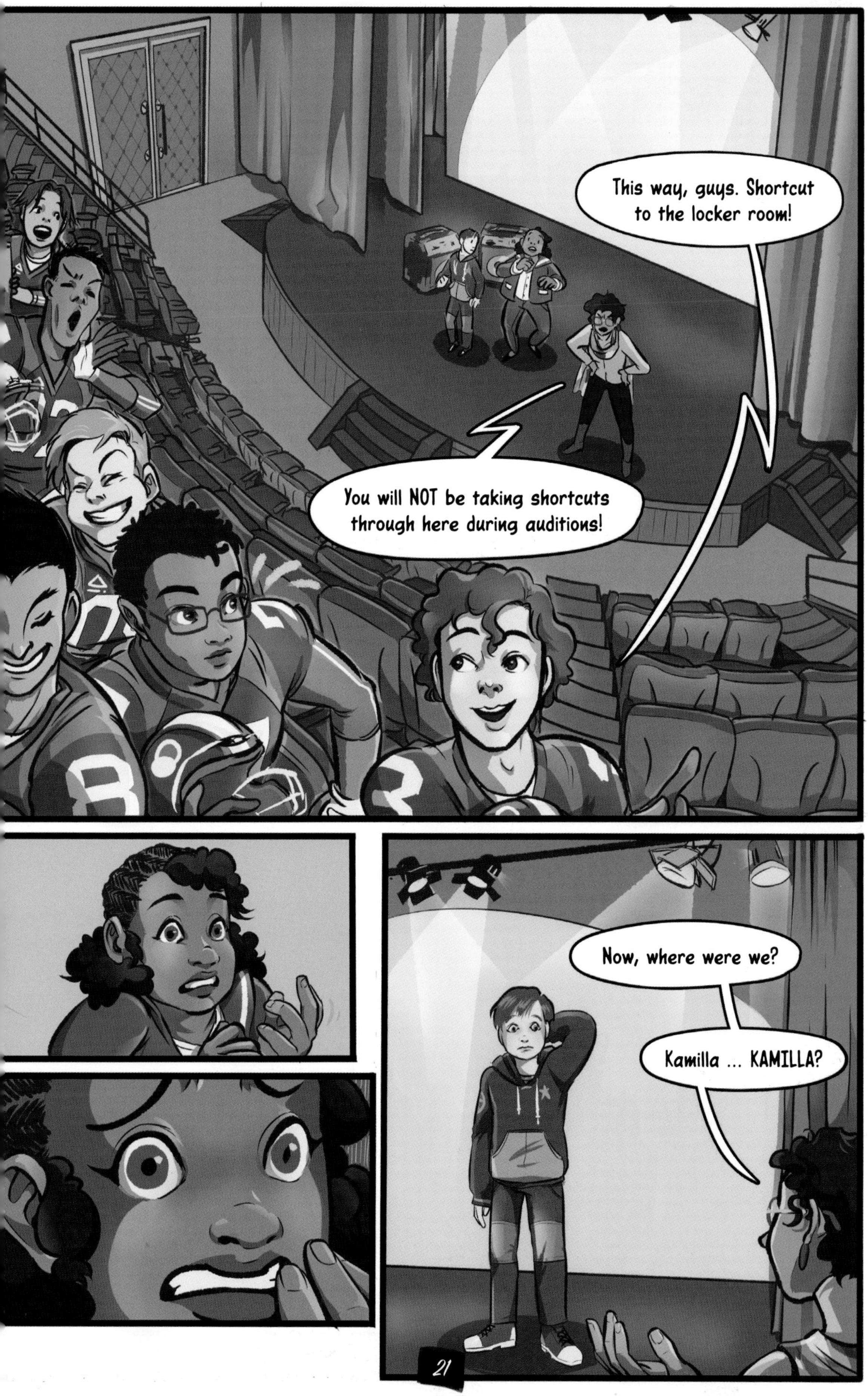
This way, guys. Shortcut to the locker room!
You will NOT be taking shortcuts through here during auditions!
Now, where were we?
Kamilla ... KAMILLA?

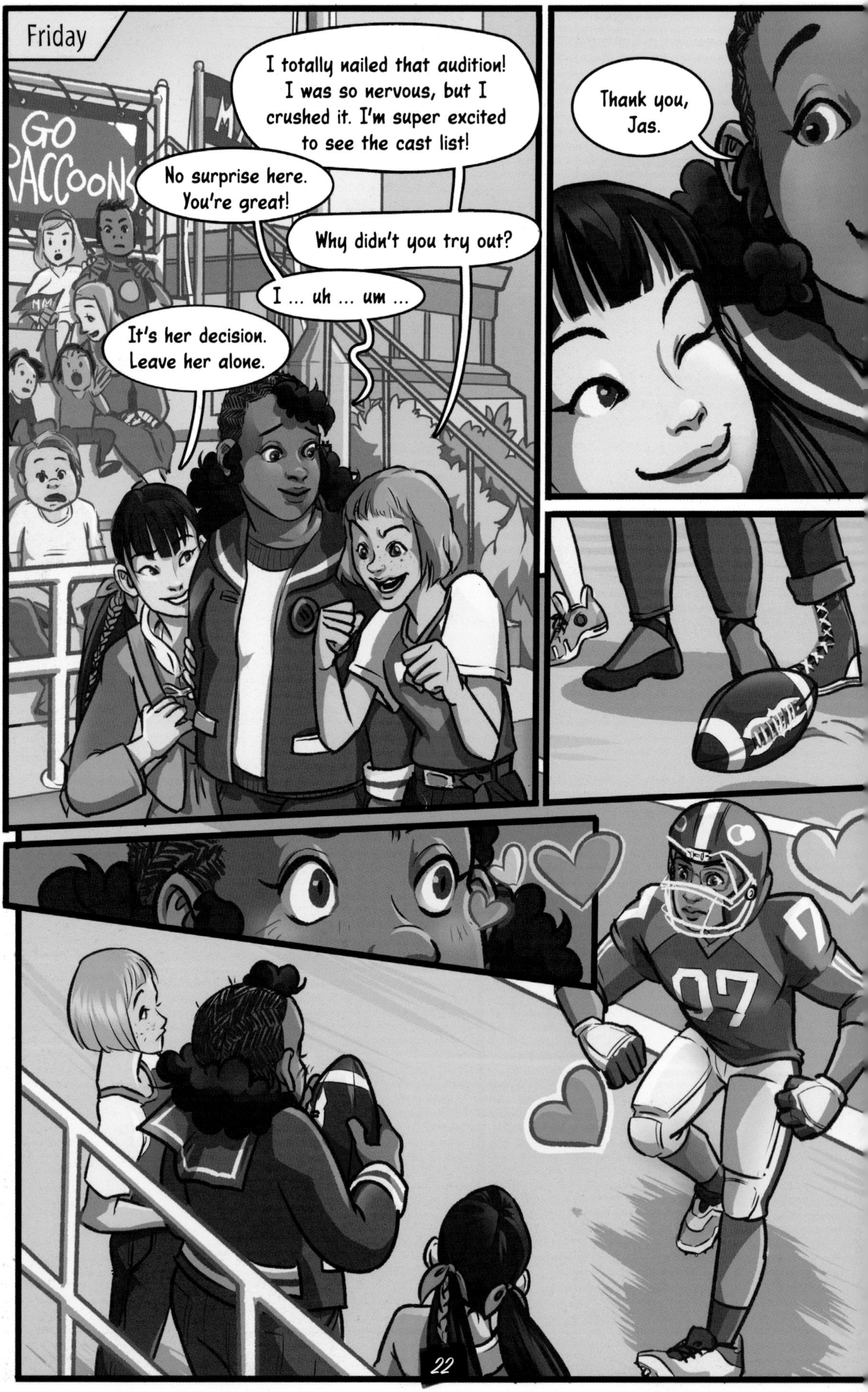
Friday
GO RACCOONS
I totally nailed that audition! I was so nervous, but I crushed it. I'm super excited to see the cast list!
No surprise here. You're great!
Why didn't you try out?
I ... uh ... um ...
It's her decision. Leave her alone.
Thank you, Jas.
07

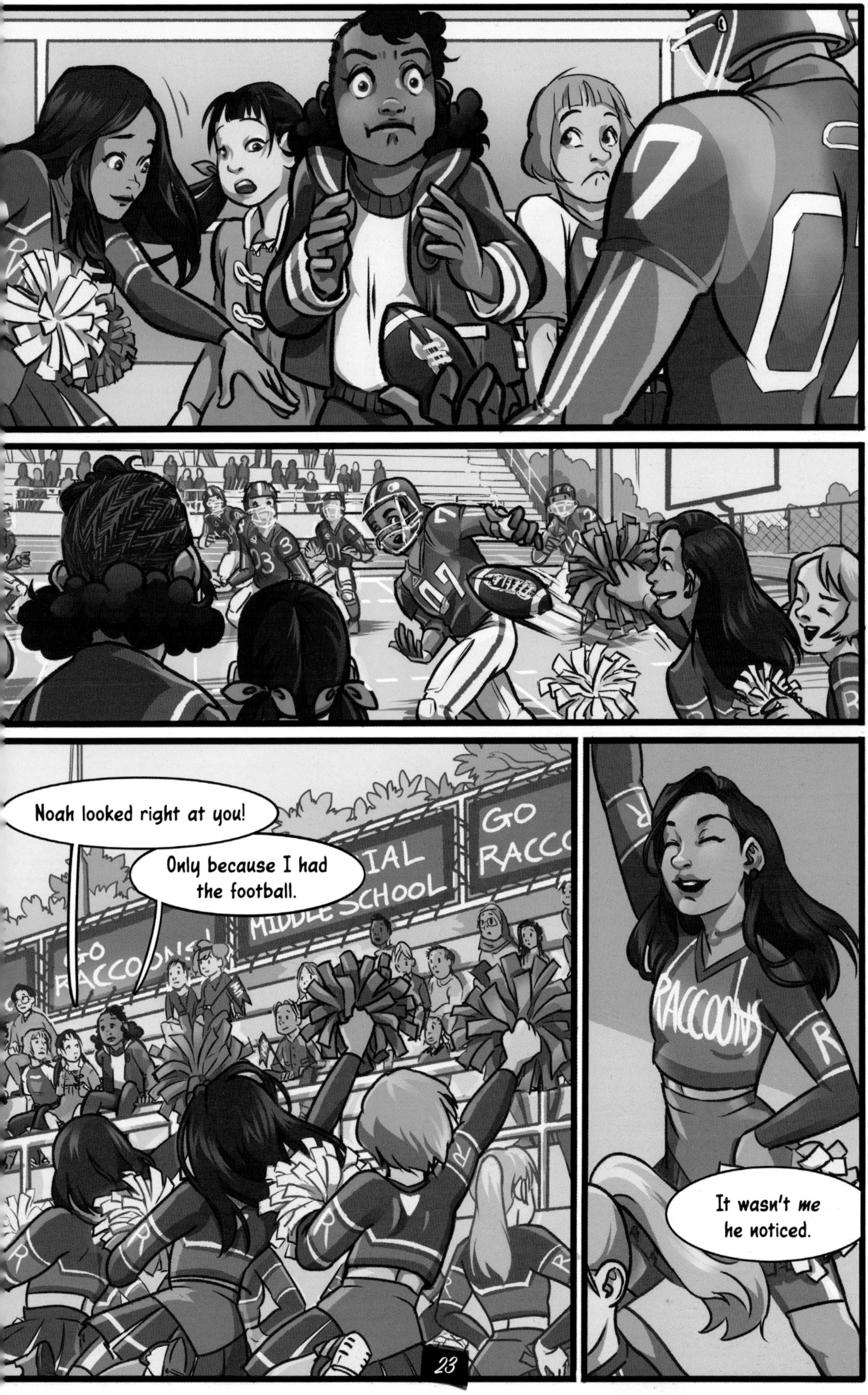
Noah looked right at you!
Only because I had the football.
MIDDLE SCHOOL
RACCOONS
It wasn't *me* he noticed.

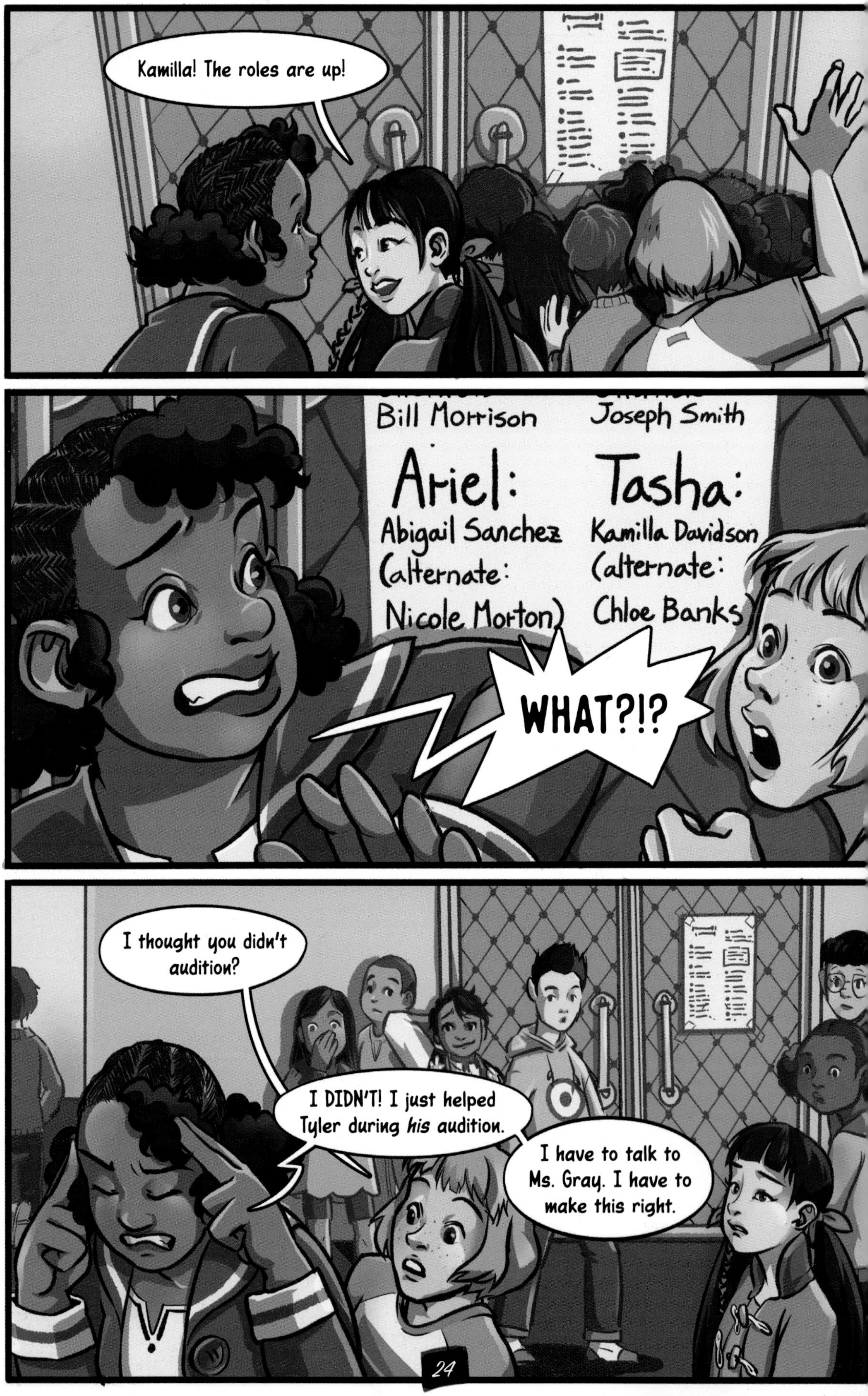
Kamilla! The roles are up!
Bill Morrison
Joseph Smith
Ariel:
Abigail Sanchez
(alternate:
Nicole Morton)
Tasha:
Kamilla Davidson
(alternate:
Chloe Banks
WHAT?!?
I thought you didn't audition?
I DIDN'T! I just helped Tyler during *his* audition.
I have to talk to Ms. Gray. I have to make this right.

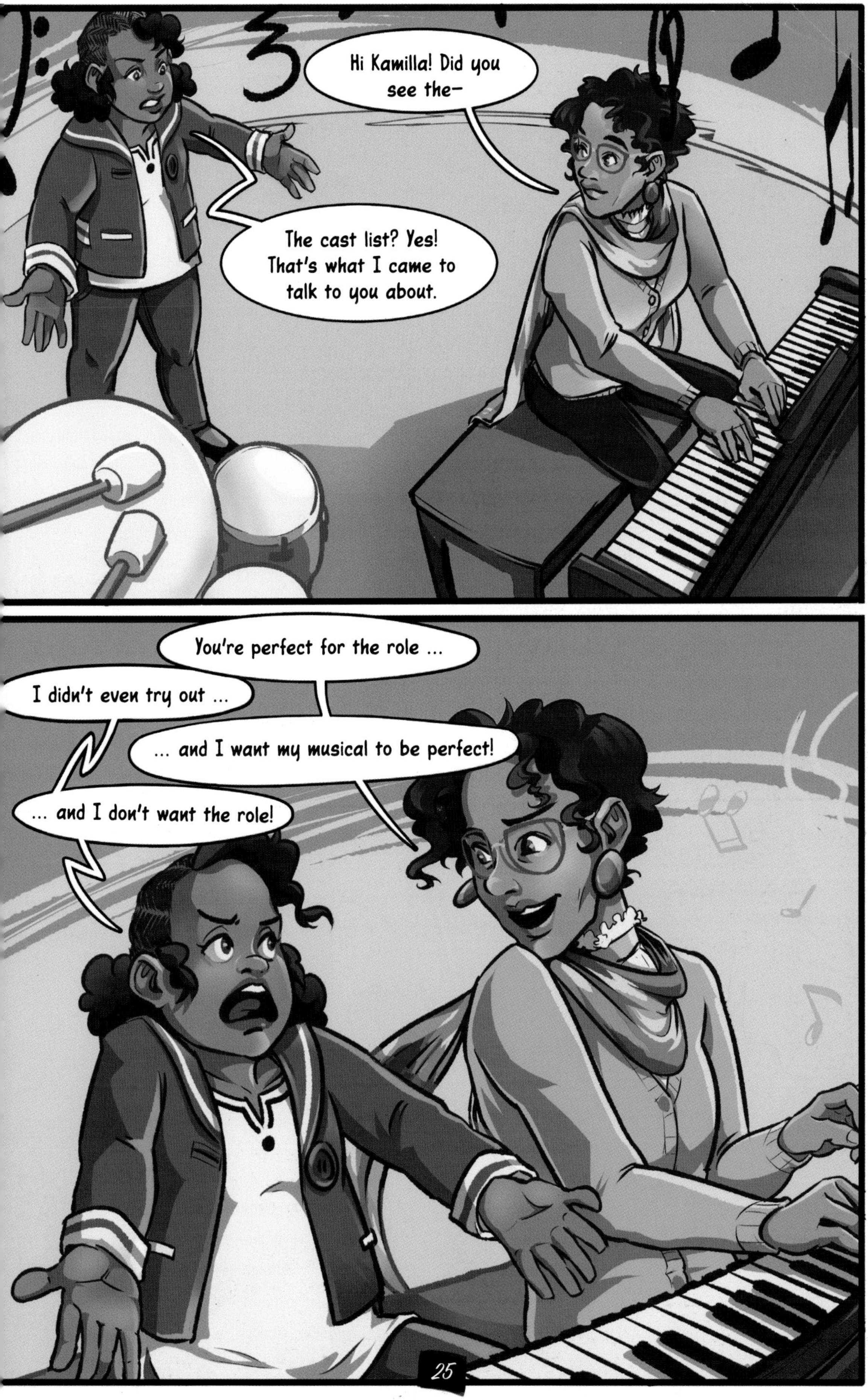
Hi Kamilla! Did you see the–
The cast list? Yes! That's what I came to talk to you about.
You're perfect for the role ...
I didn't even try out ...
... and I want my musical to be perfect!
... and I don't want the role!

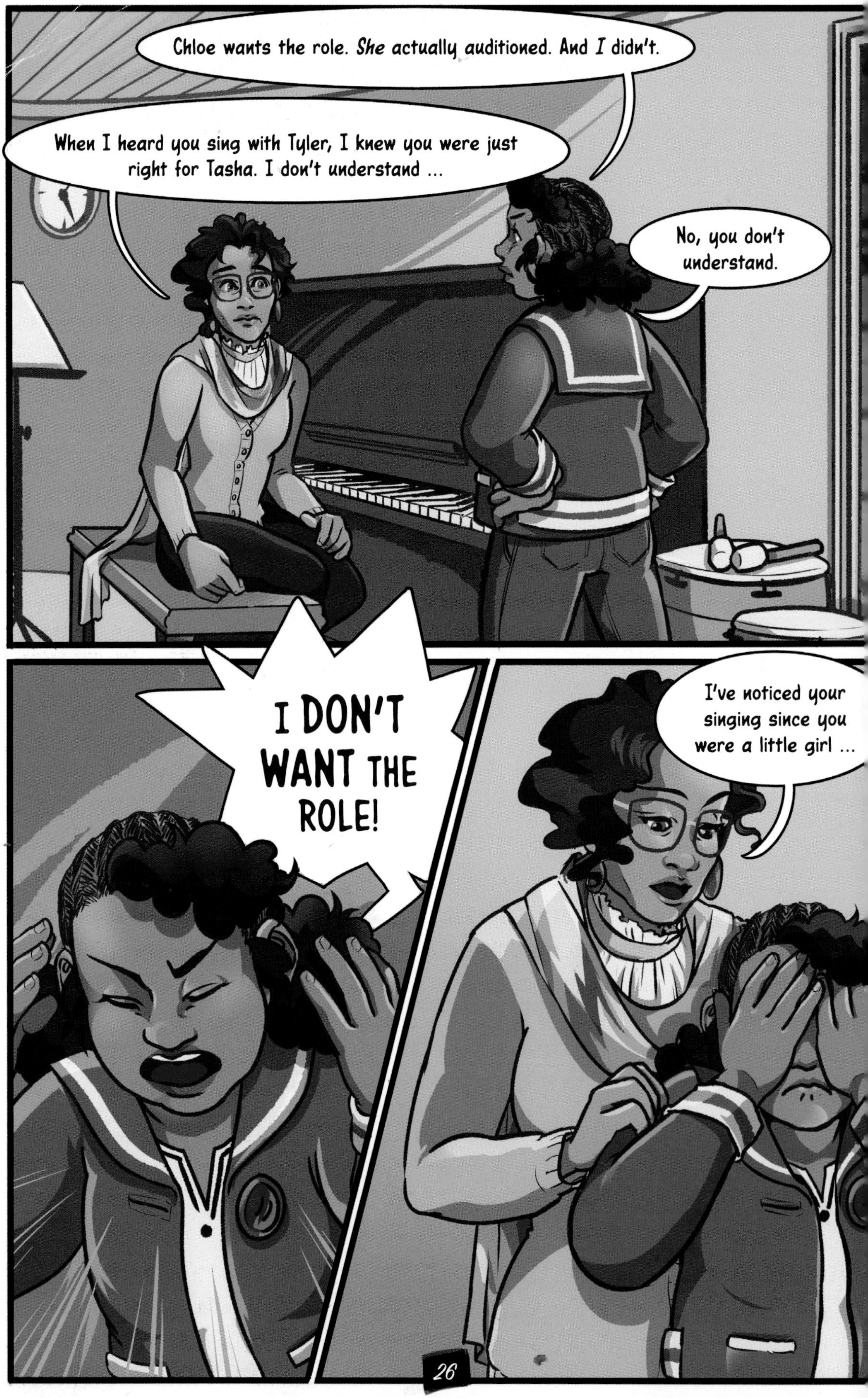
Chloe wants the role. *She* actually auditioned. And *I* didn't.
When I heard you sing with Tyler, I knew you were just right for Tasha. I don't understand ...
No, you don't understand.
I DON'T WANT THE ROLE!
I've noticed your singing since you were a little girl ...

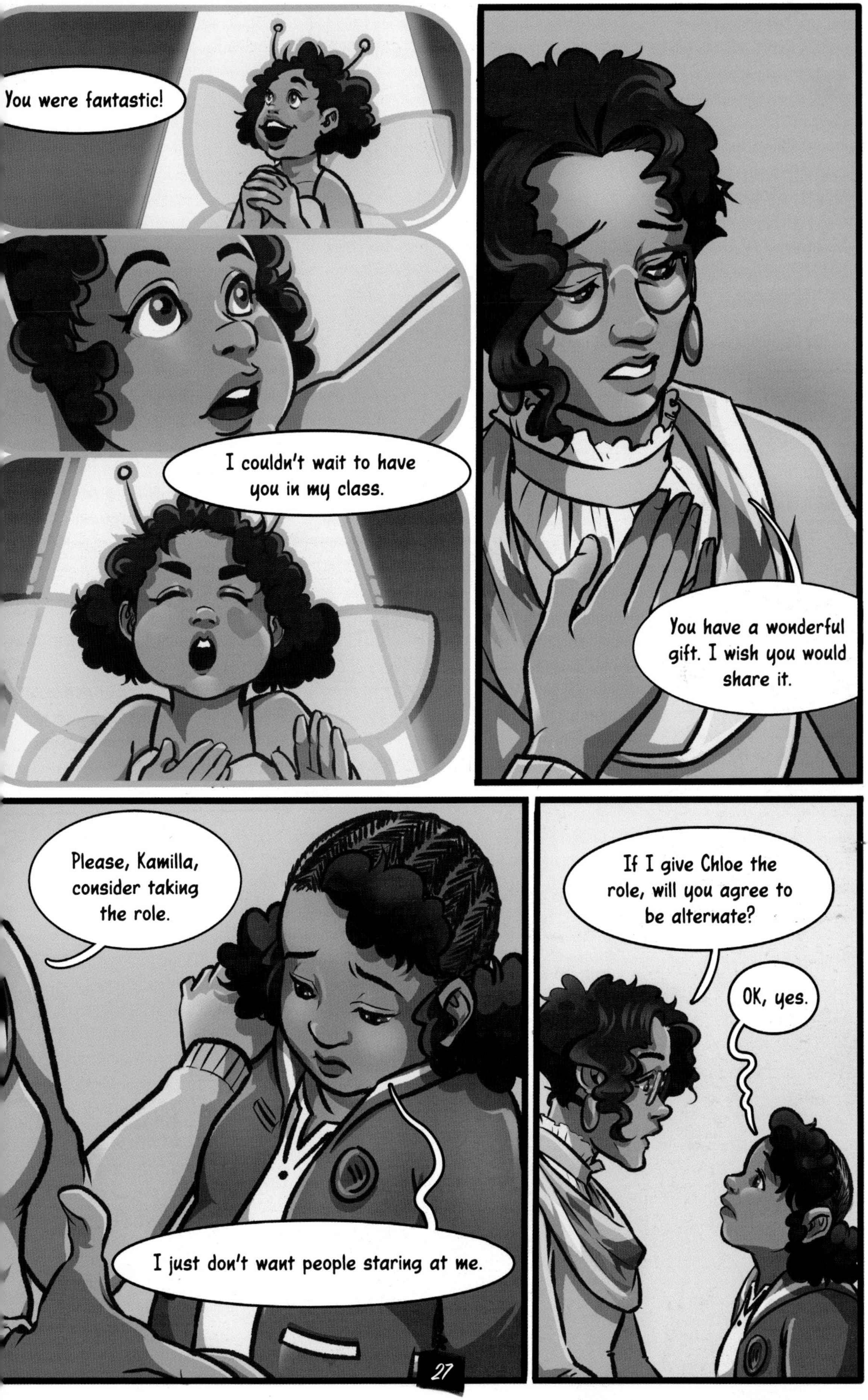
You were fantastic!
I couldn't wait to have you in my class.
You have a wonderful gift. I wish you would share it.
Please, Kamilla, consider taking the role.
I just don't want people staring at me.
If I give Chloe the role, will you agree to be alternate?
OK, yes.

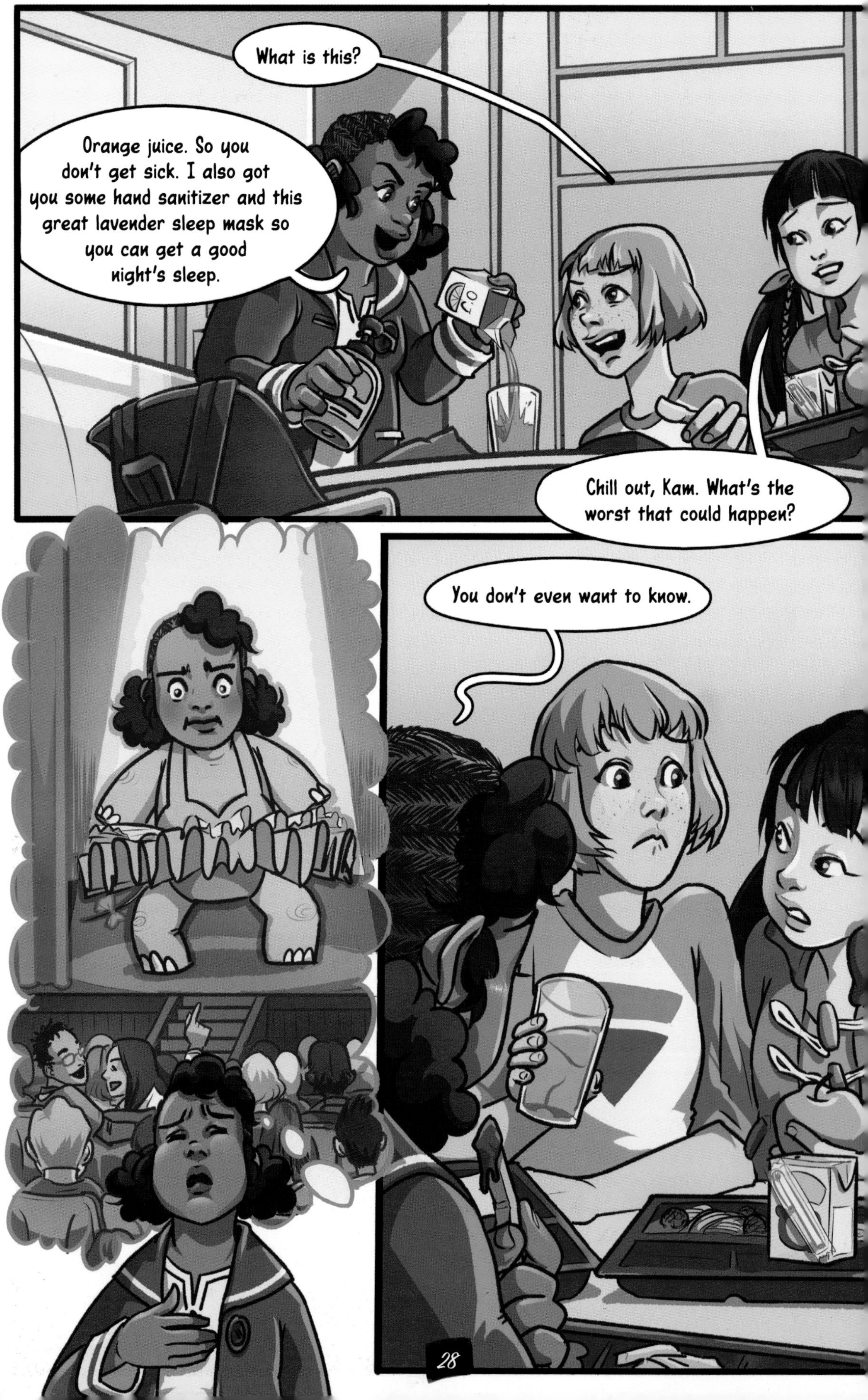
What is this?
Orange juice. So you don't get sick. I also got you some hand sanitizer and this great lavender sleep mask so you can get a good night's sleep.
Chill out, Kam. What's the worst that could happen?
You don't even want to know.

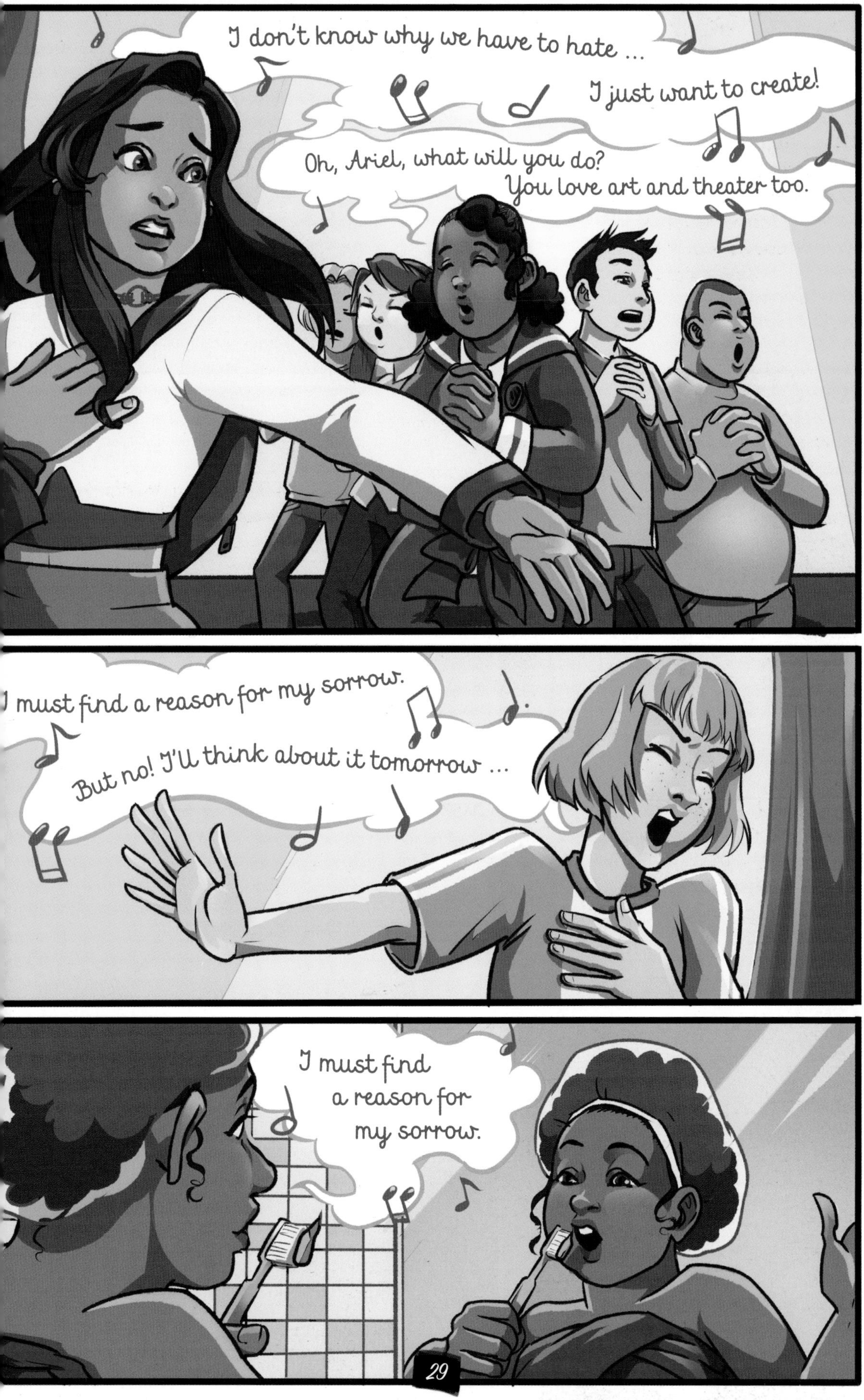
I don't know why we have to hate ...
I just want to create!
Oh, Ariel, what will you do?
You love art and theater too.
I must find a reason for my sorrow.
But no! I'll think about it tomorrow ...
I must find a reason for my sorrow.

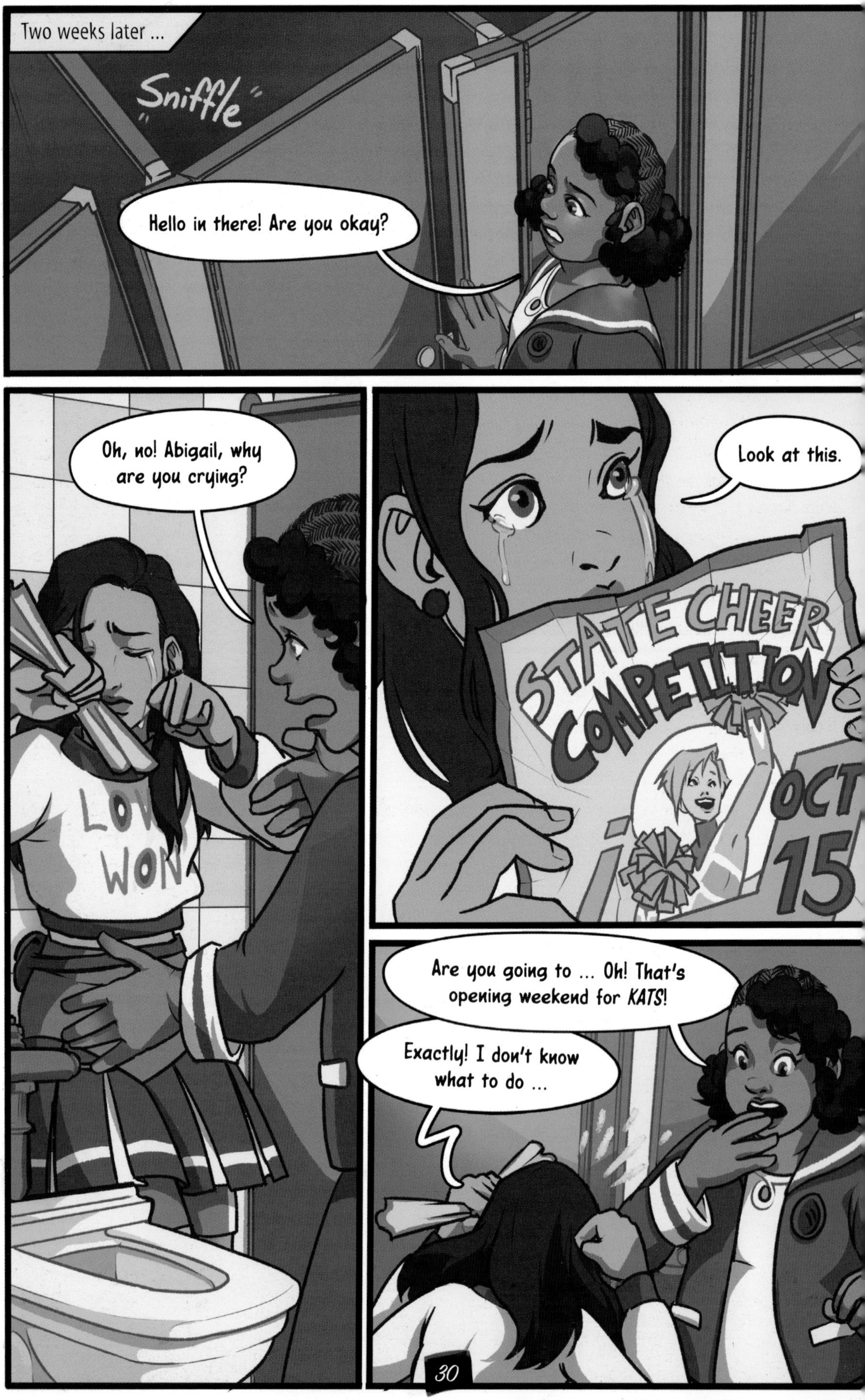
Two weeks later ...
Sniffle
Hello in there! Are you okay?
Oh, no! Abigail, why are you crying?
Look at this.
STATE CHEER COMPETITION
OCT 15
Are you going to ... Oh! That's opening weekend for *KATS*!
Exactly! I don't know what to do ...

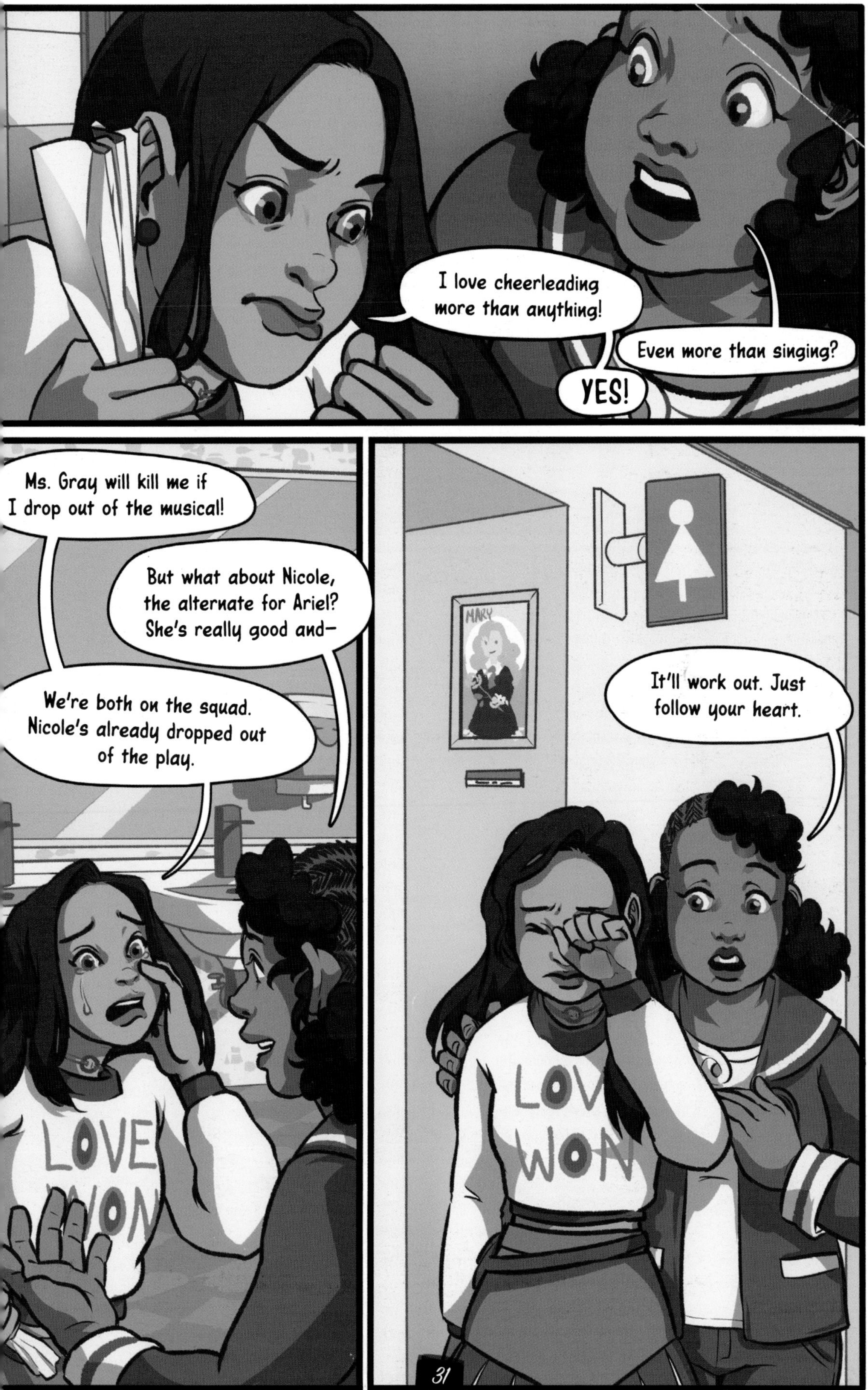
I love cheerleading more than anything!
Even more than singing?
YES!
Ms. Gray will kill me if I drop out of the musical!
But what about Nicole, the alternate for Ariel? She's really good and—
We're both on the squad. Nicole's already dropped out of the play.
MARY
It'll work out. Just follow your heart.
LOVE WON

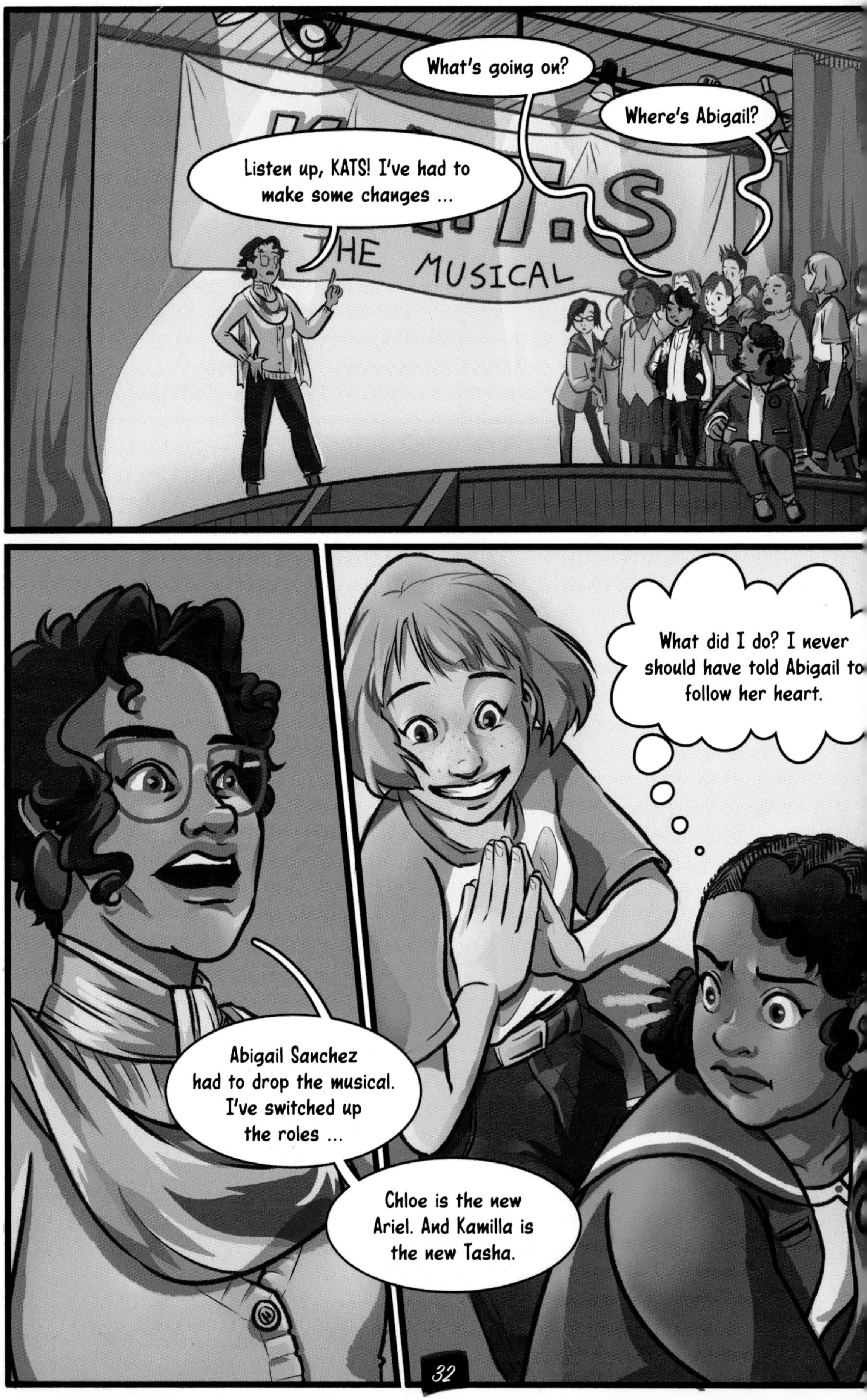
What's going on?
Where's Abigail?
Listen up, KATS! I've had to make some changes ...
THE MUSICAL
What did I do? I never should have told Abigail to follow her heart.
Abigail Sanchez had to drop the musical. I've switched up the roles ...
Chloe is the new Ariel. And Kamilla is the new Tasha.

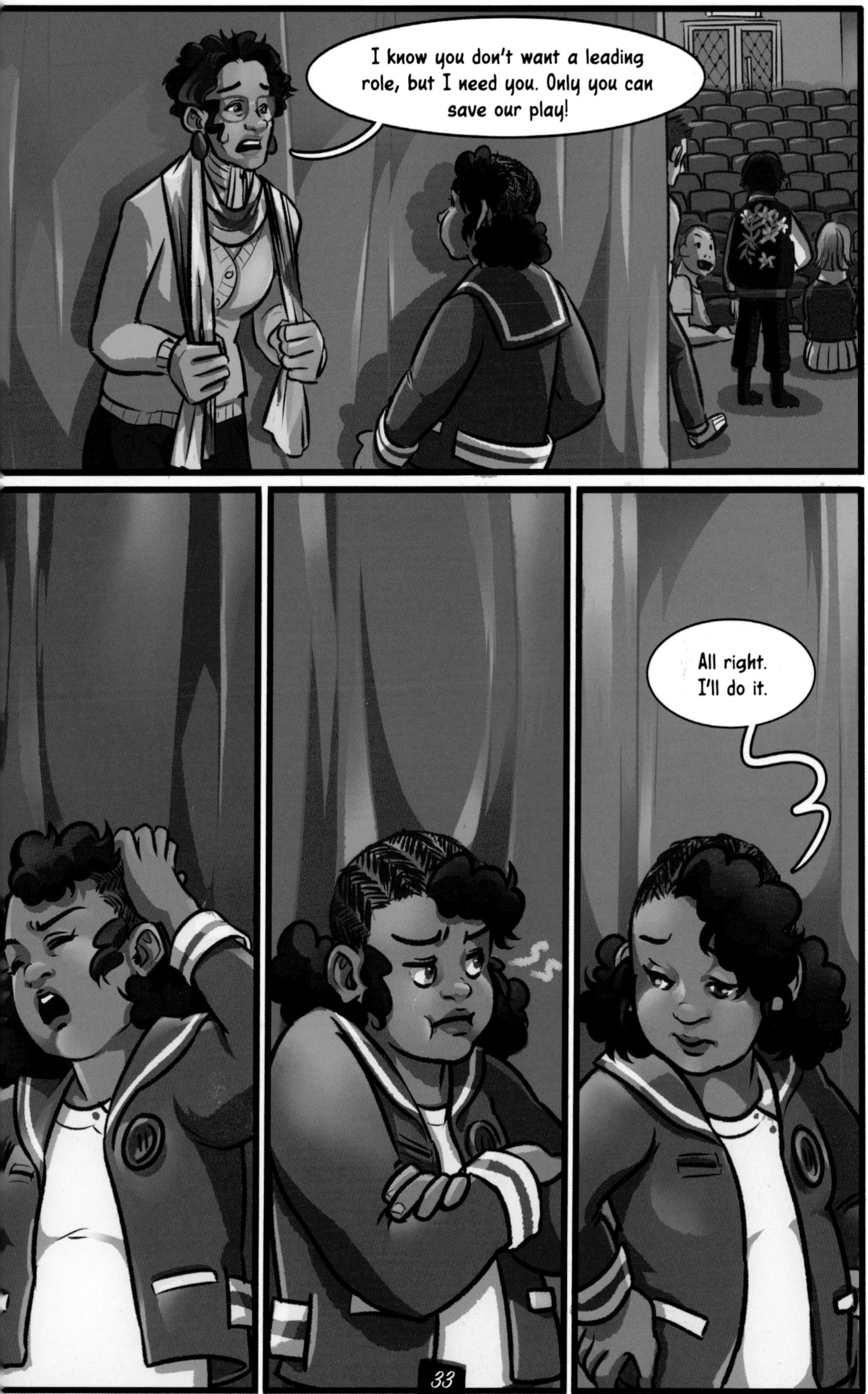
I know you don't want a leading role, but I need you. Only you can save our play!
All right. I'll do it.

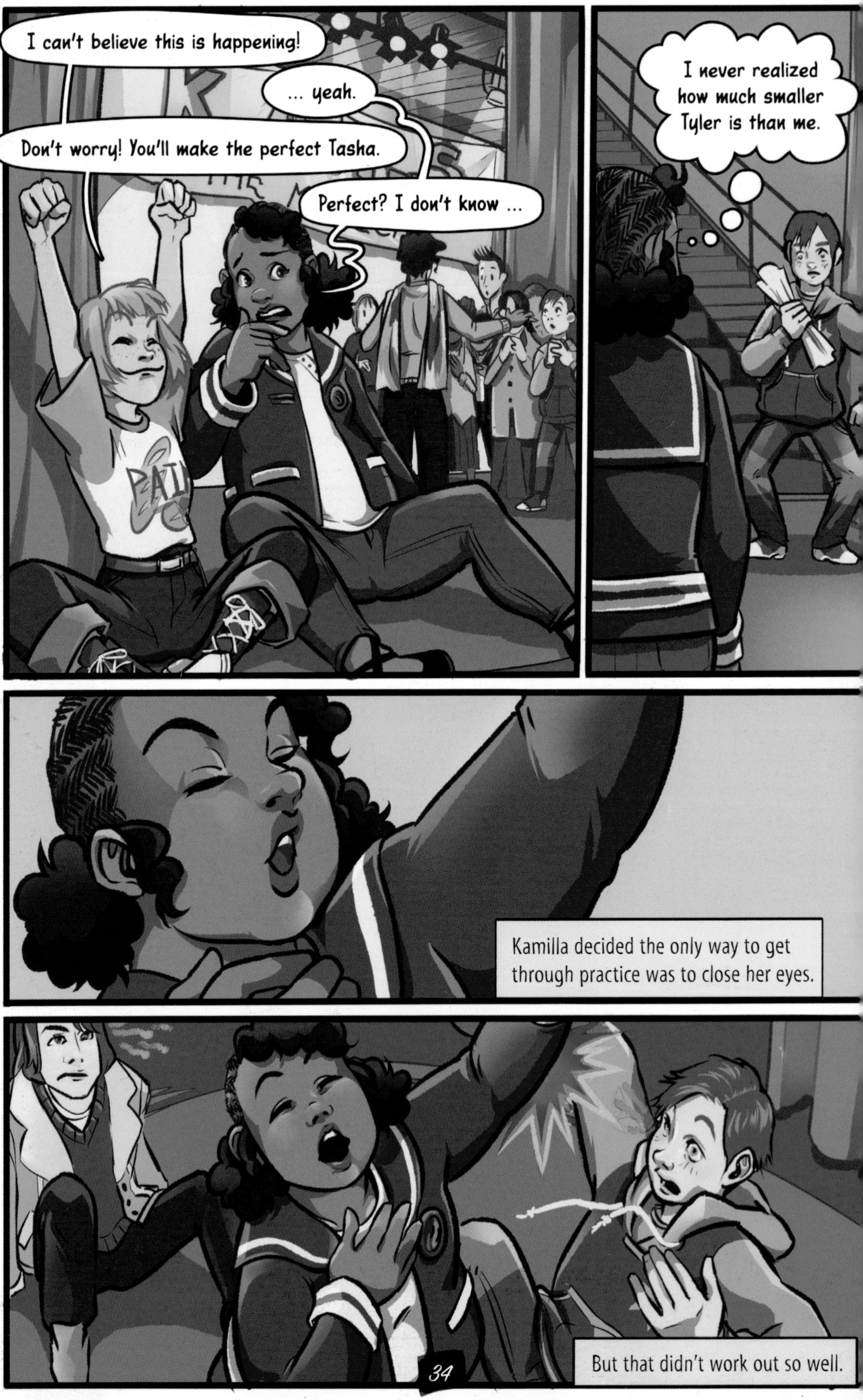
I can't believe this is happening!
... yeah.
Don't worry! You'll make the perfect Tasha.
Perfect? I don't know ...
I never realized how much smaller Tyler is than me.
Kamilla decided the only way to get through practice was to close her eyes.
But that didn't work out so well.

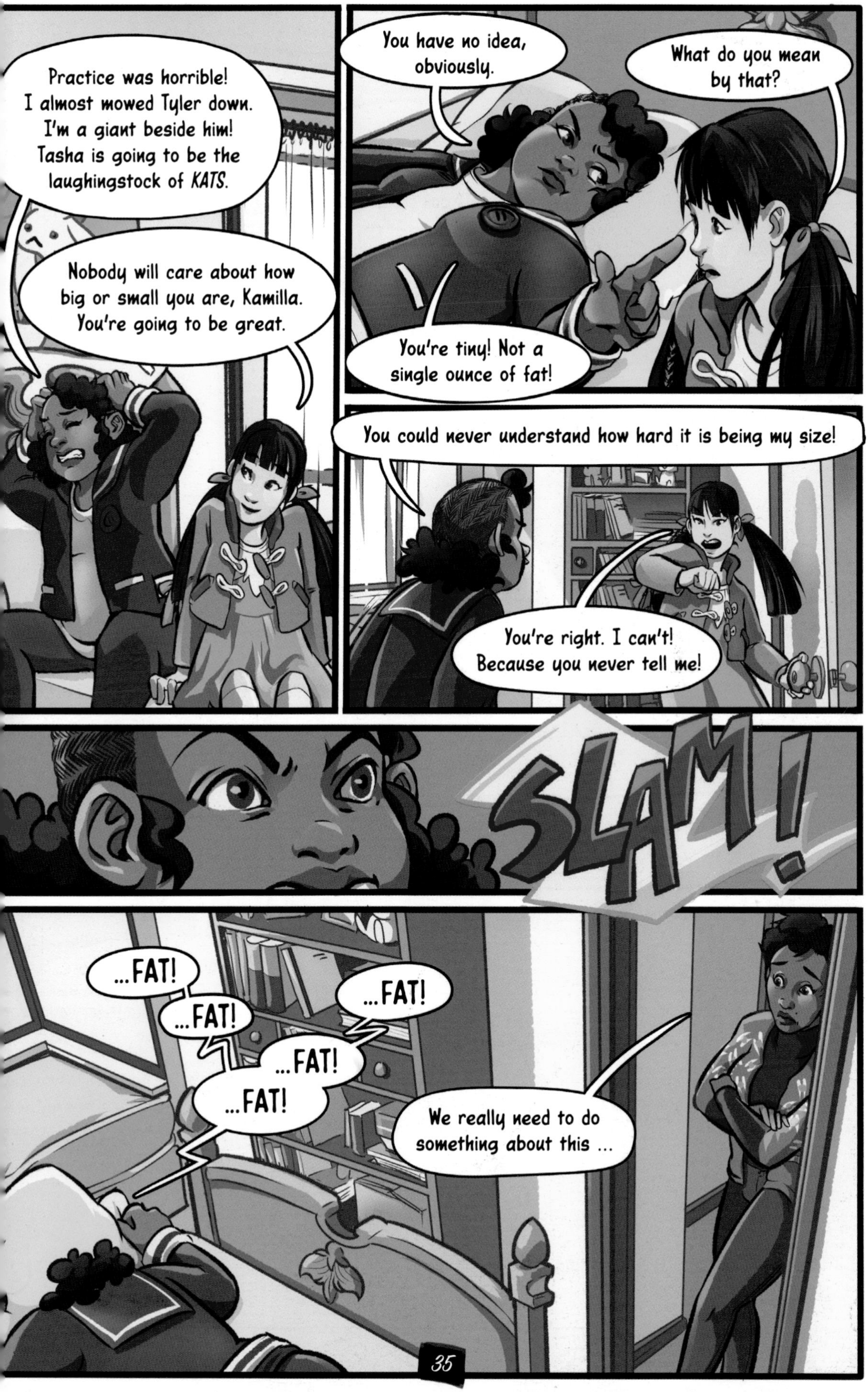
Practice was horrible! I almost mowed Tyler down. I'm a giant beside him! Tasha is going to be the laughingstock of *KATS*.
Nobody will care about how big or small you are, Kamilla. You're going to be great.
You have no idea, obviously.
What do you mean by that?
You're tiny! Not a single ounce of fat!
You could never understand how hard it is being my size!
You're right. I can't! Because you never tell me!
SLAM!
...FAT!
...FAT!
...FAT!
...FAT!
...FAT!
We really need to do something about this ...

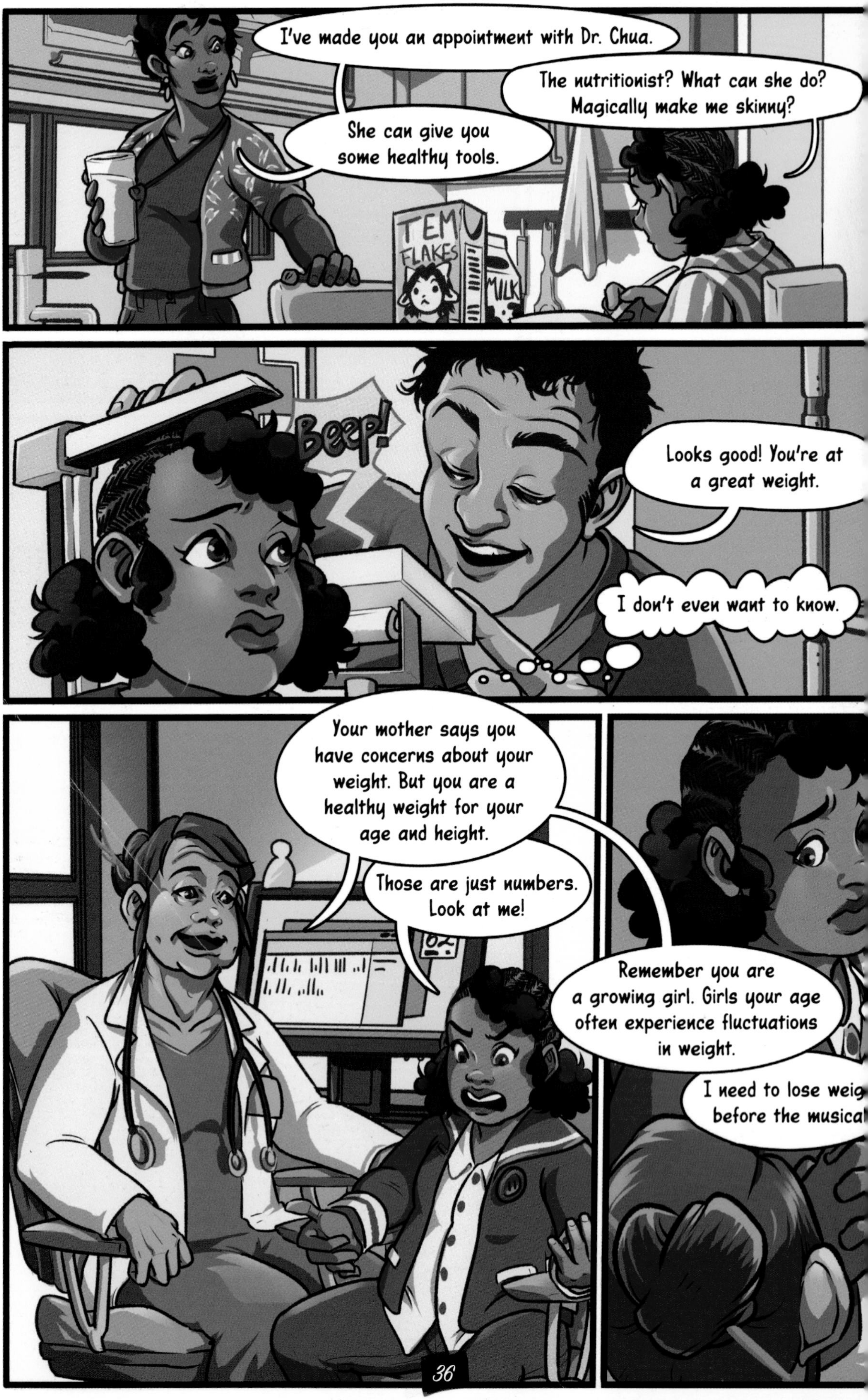
I've made you an appointment with Dr. Chua.
The nutritionist? What can she do? Magically make me skinny?
She can give you some healthy tools.
TEM FLAKES
MILK
Beep!
Looks good! You're at a great weight.
I don't even want to know.
Your mother says you have concerns about your weight. But you are a healthy weight for your age and height.
Those are just numbers. Look at me!
Remember you are a growing girl. Girls your age often experience fluctuations in weight.
I need to lose weig
before the musica

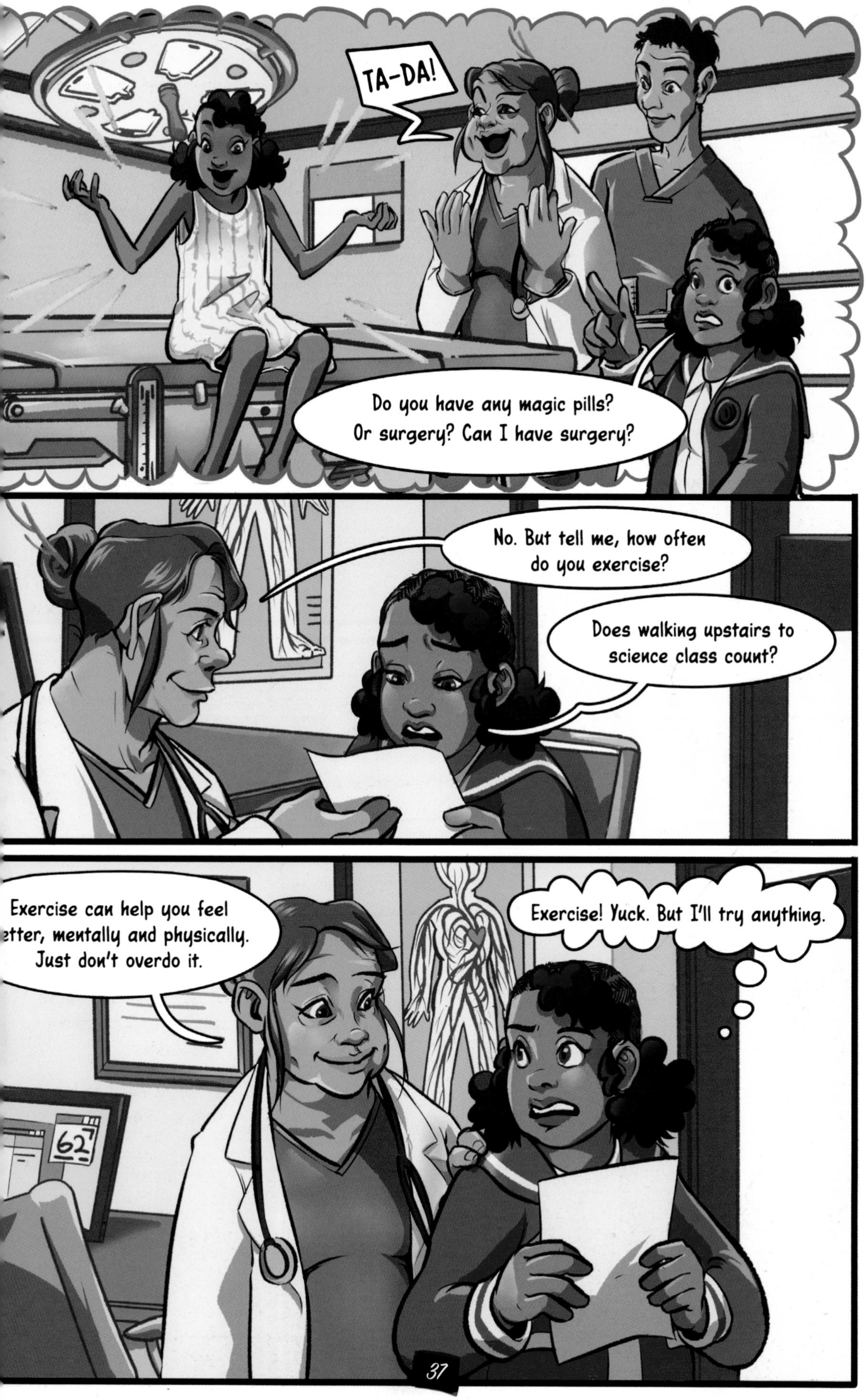
TA-DA!
Do you have any magic pills? Or surgery? Can I have surgery?
No. But tell me, how often do you exercise?
Does walking upstairs to science class count?
Exercise can help you feel etter, mentally and physically. Just don't overdo it.
Exercise! Yuck. But I'll try anything.
62

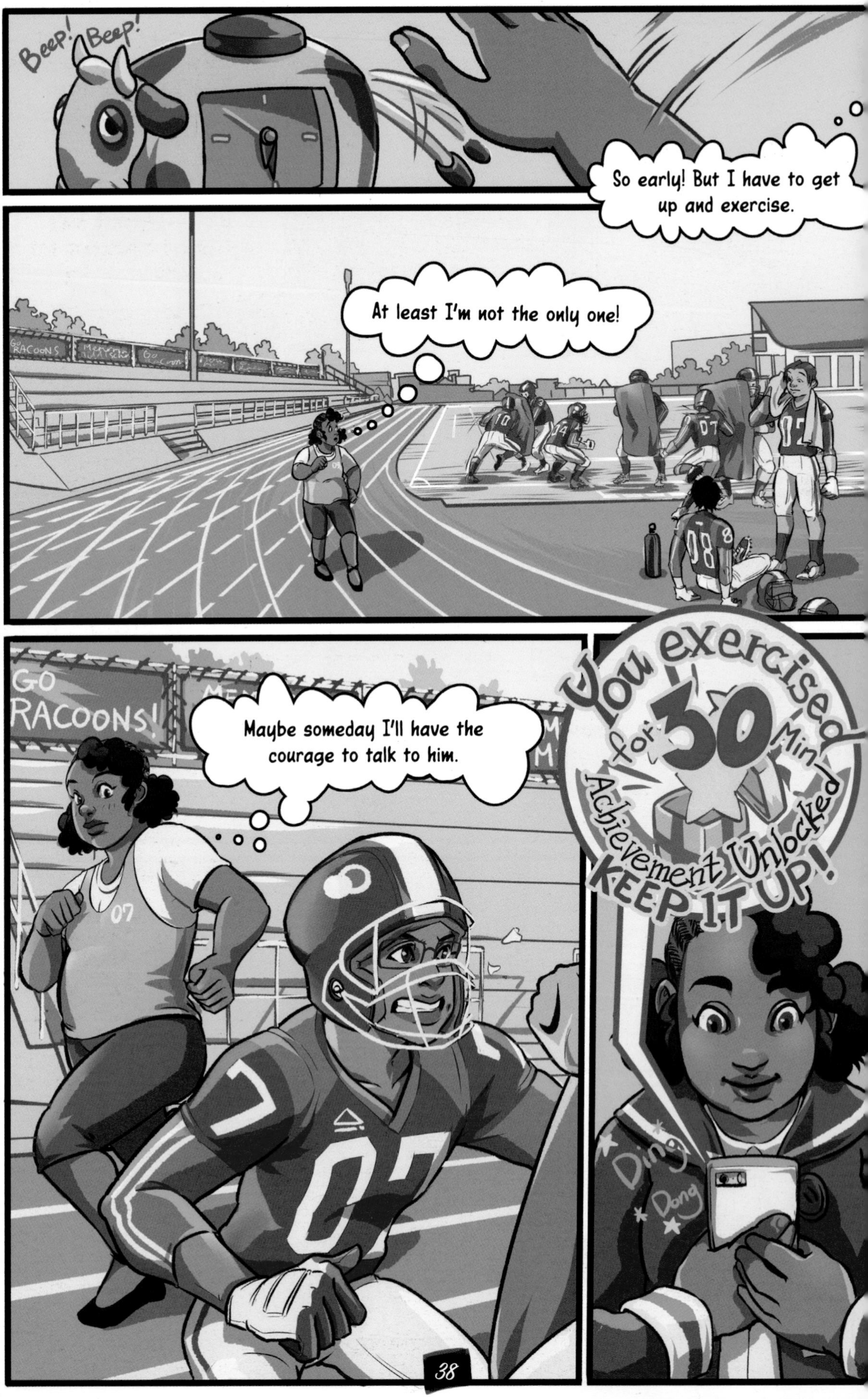
Beep! Beep!
So early! But I have to get up and exercise.
GO RACOONS
At least I'm not the only one!
GO RACOONS!
Maybe someday I'll have the courage to talk to him.
You exercised for 30 Min
Achievement Unlocked
KEEP IT UP!
Ding Dong

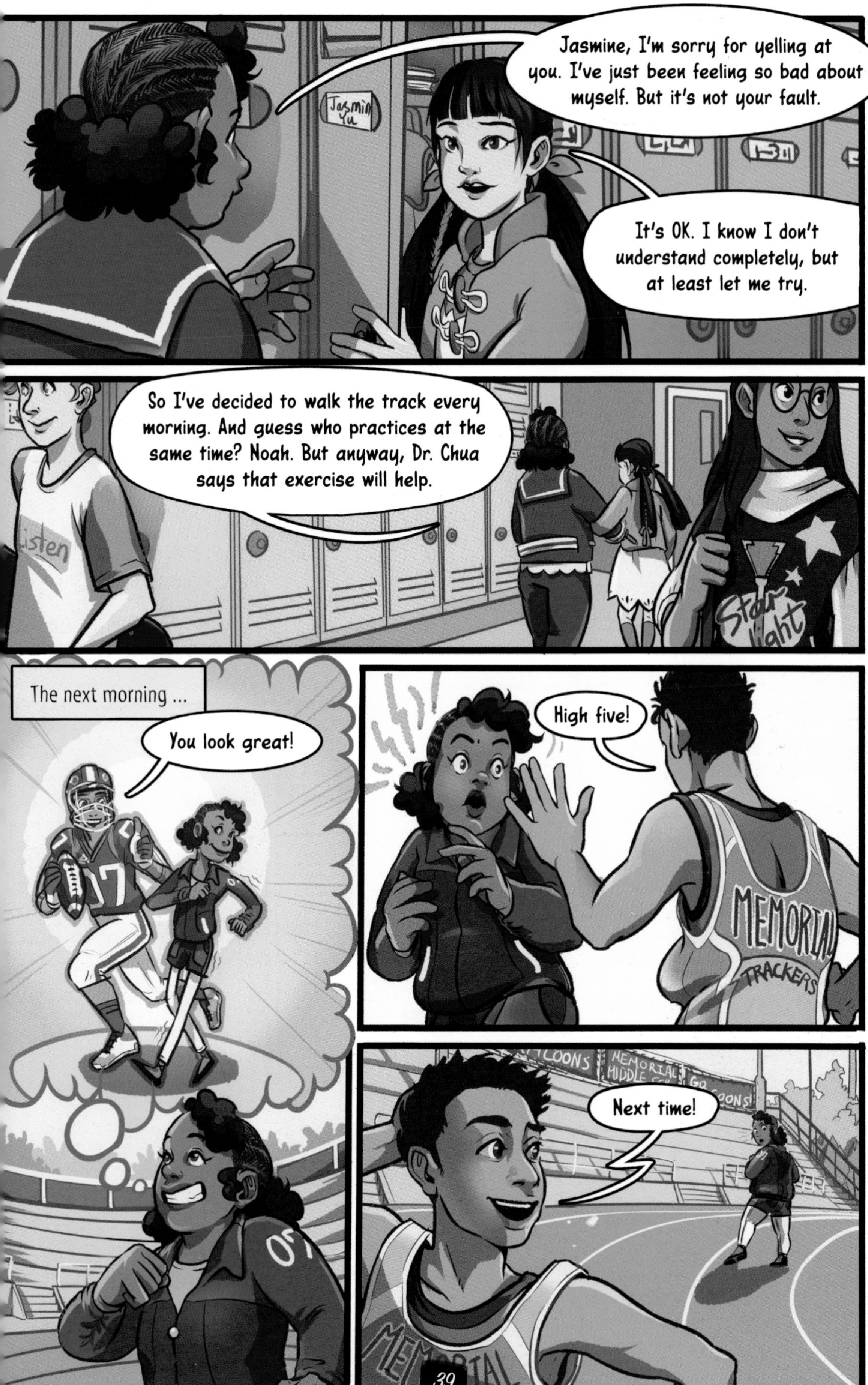
Jasmin Yu
Jasmine, I'm sorry for yelling at you. I've just been feeling so bad about myself. But it's not your fault.
It's OK. I know I don't understand completely, but at least let me try.
Listen
So I've decided to walk the track every morning. And guess who practices at the same time? Noah. But anyway, Dr. Chua says that exercise will help.
Star light
The next morning ...
You look great!
High five!
MEMORIAL
TRACKERS
Next time!

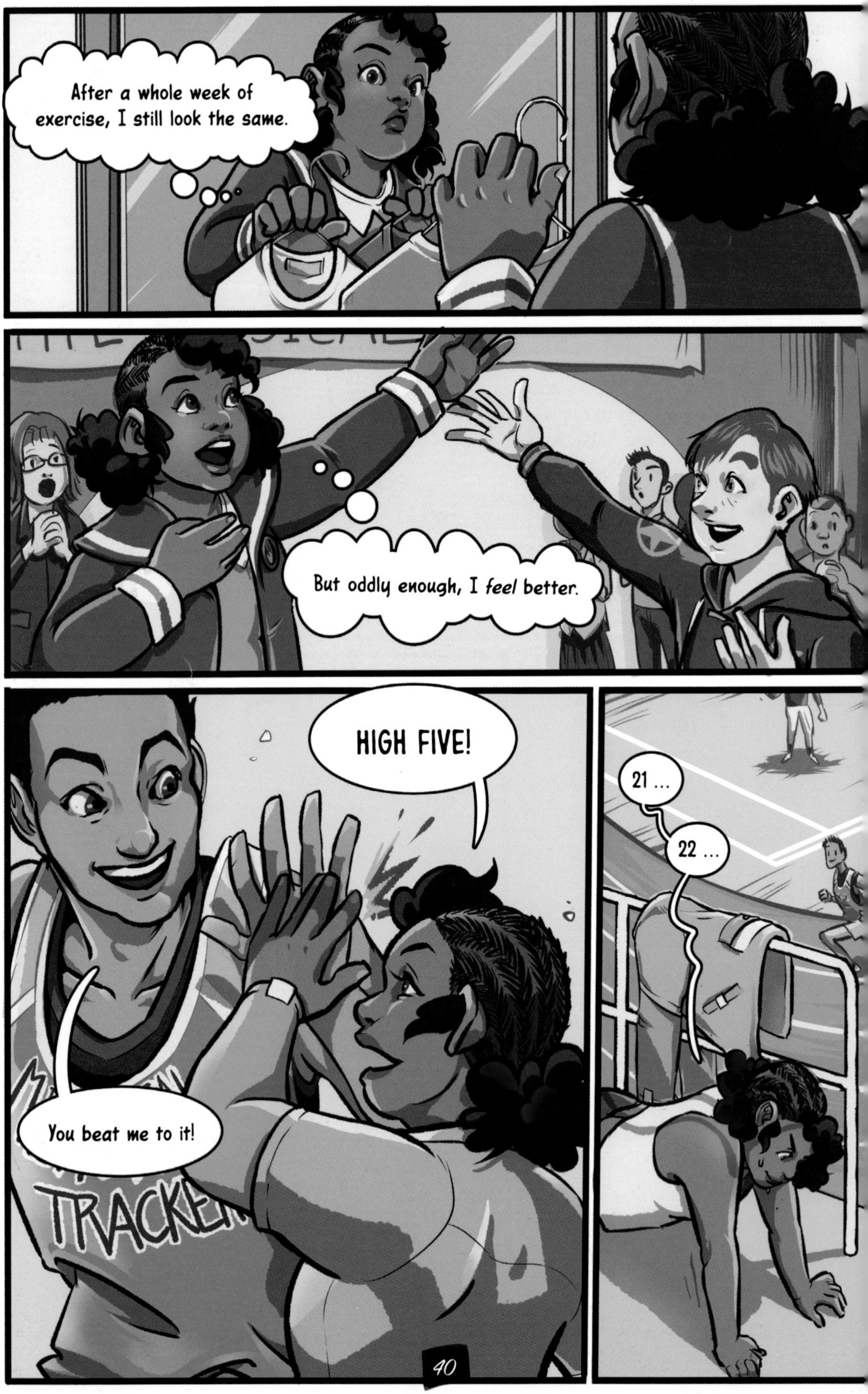
After a whole week of exercise, I still look the same.
But oddly enough, I *feel* better.
HIGH FIVE!
You beat me to it!
TRACKE
21 ...
22 ...

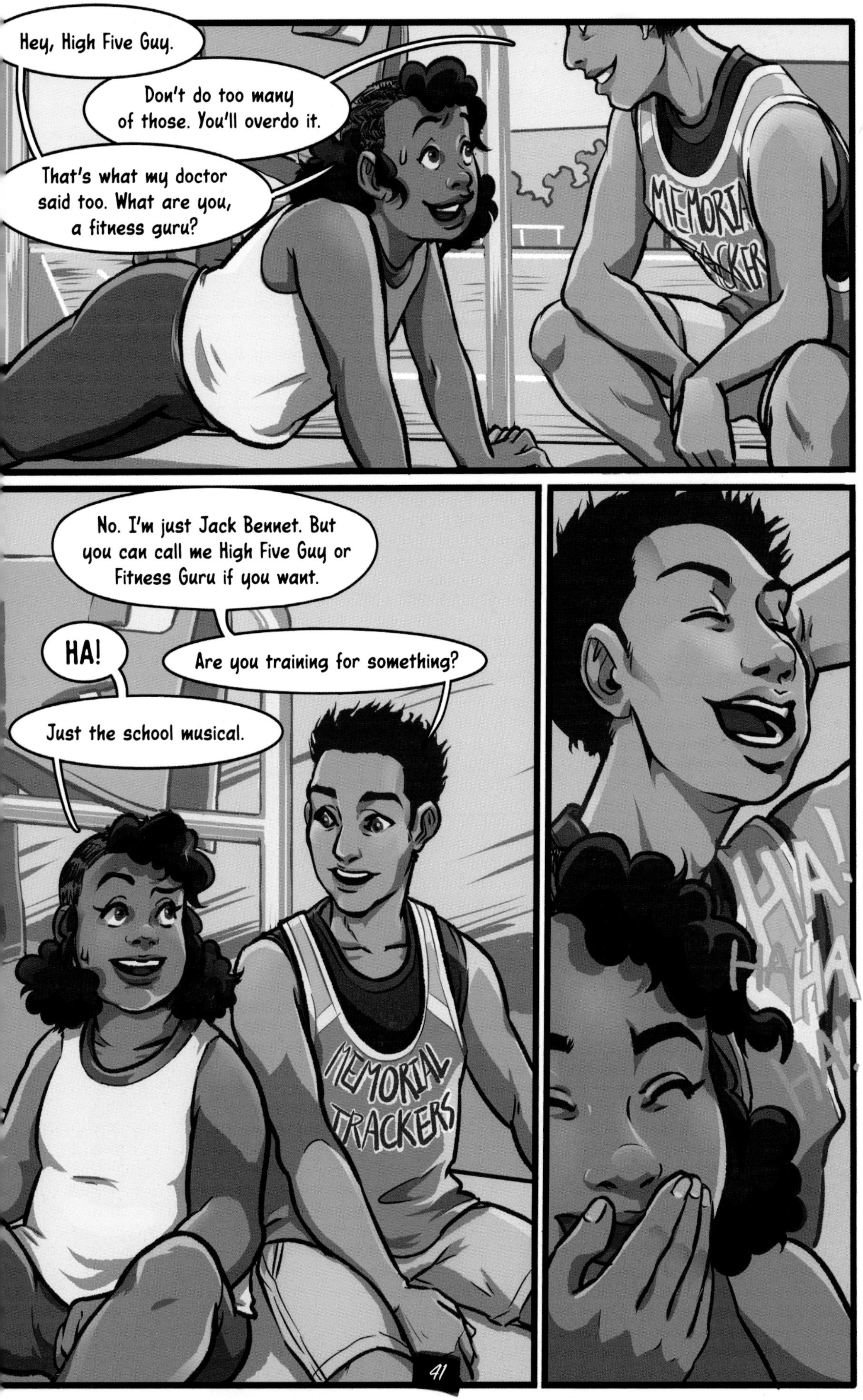

Hey, High Five Guy.
Don't do too many of those. You'll overdo it.
That's what my doctor said too. What are you, a fitness guru?
No. I'm just Jack Bennet. But you can call me High Five Guy or Fitness Guru if you want.
HA!
Are you training for something?
Just the school musical.
MEMORIAL TRACKERS
HA!
HAHA
HA!

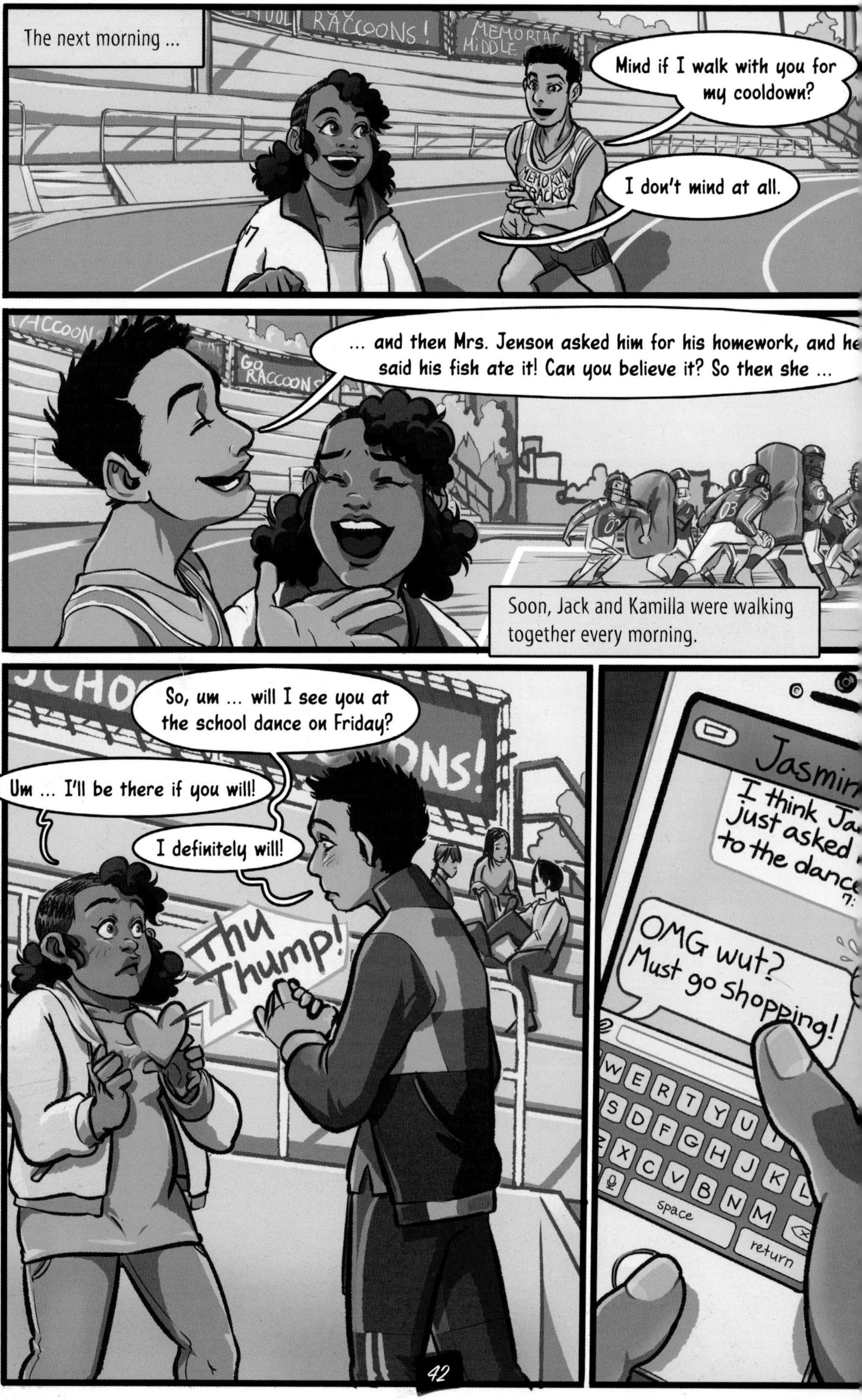

The next morning ...
Mind if I walk with you for my cooldown?
I don't mind at all.
... and then Mrs. Jenson asked him for his homework, and he said his fish ate it! Can you believe it? So then she ...
Soon, Jack and Kamilla were walking together every morning.
So, um ... will I see you at the school dance on Friday?
Um ... I'll be there if you will!
I definitely will!
Thu Thump!
OMG wut? Must go shopping!

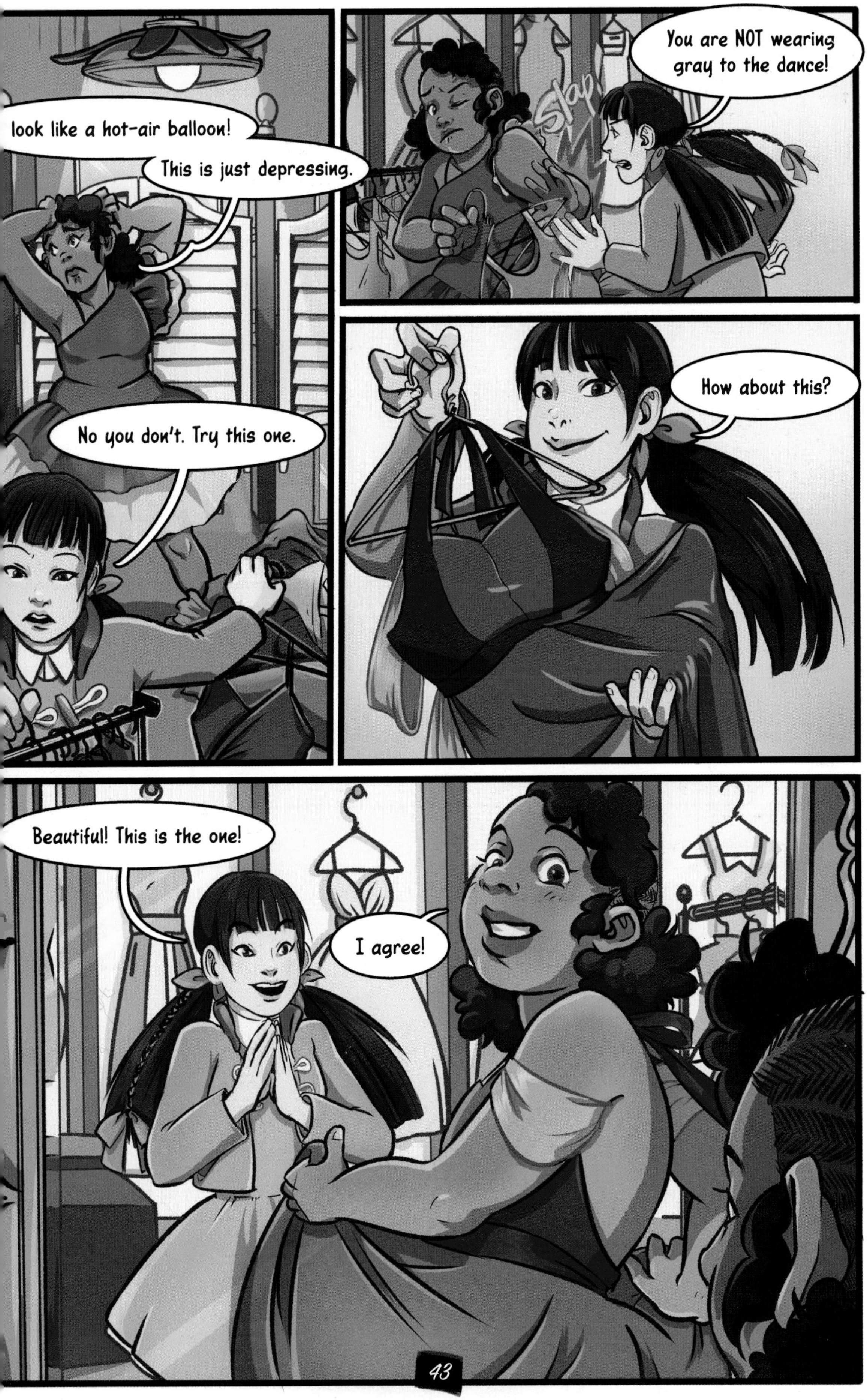
look like a hot-air balloon!
This is just depressing.
No you don't. Try this one.
slap!
You are NOT wearing gray to the dance!
How about this?
Beautiful! This is the one!
I agree!

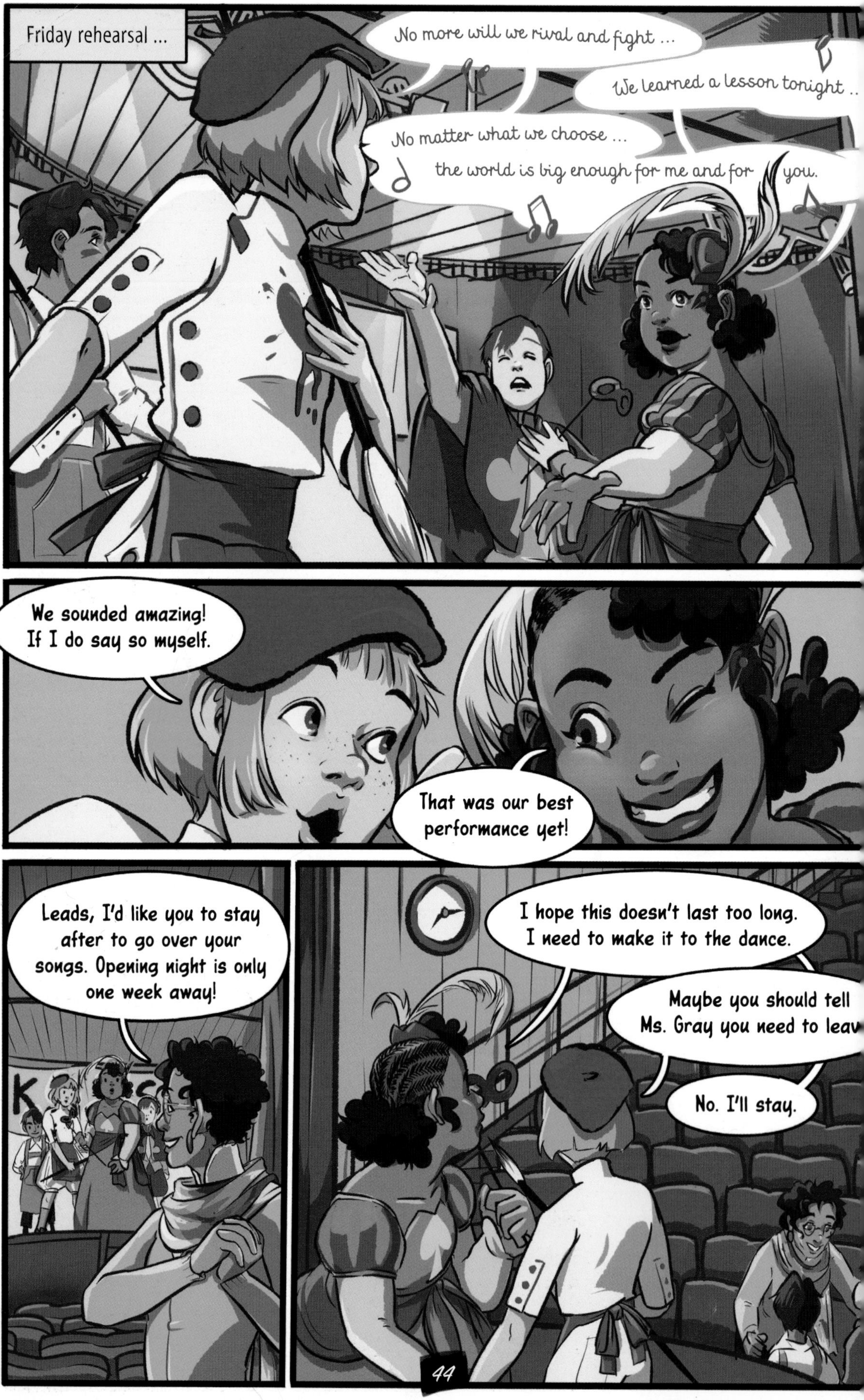

Friday rehearsal ...
No more will we rival and fight ...
We learned a lesson tonight ...
No matter what we choose ...
the world is big enough for me and for you.
We sounded amazing! If I do say so myself.
That was our best performance yet!
Leads, I'd like you to stay after to go over your songs. Opening night is only one week away!
I hope this doesn't last too long. I need to make it to the dance.
Maybe you should tell Ms. Gray you need to leav
No. I'll stay.

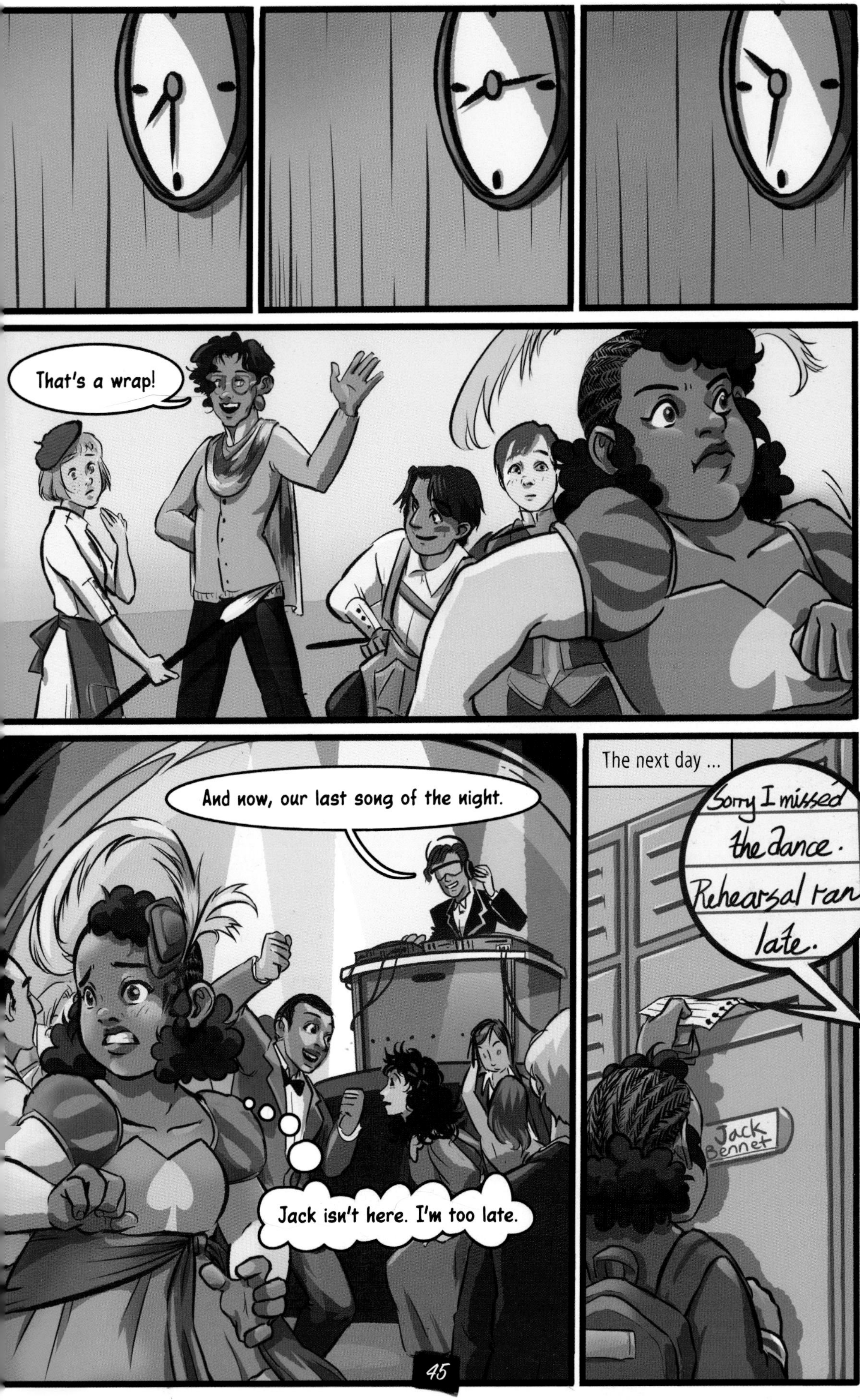
That's a wrap!
And now, our last song of the night.
Jack isn't here. I'm too late.
The next day ...
Sorry I missed the dance. Rehearsal ran late.
Jack Bennet

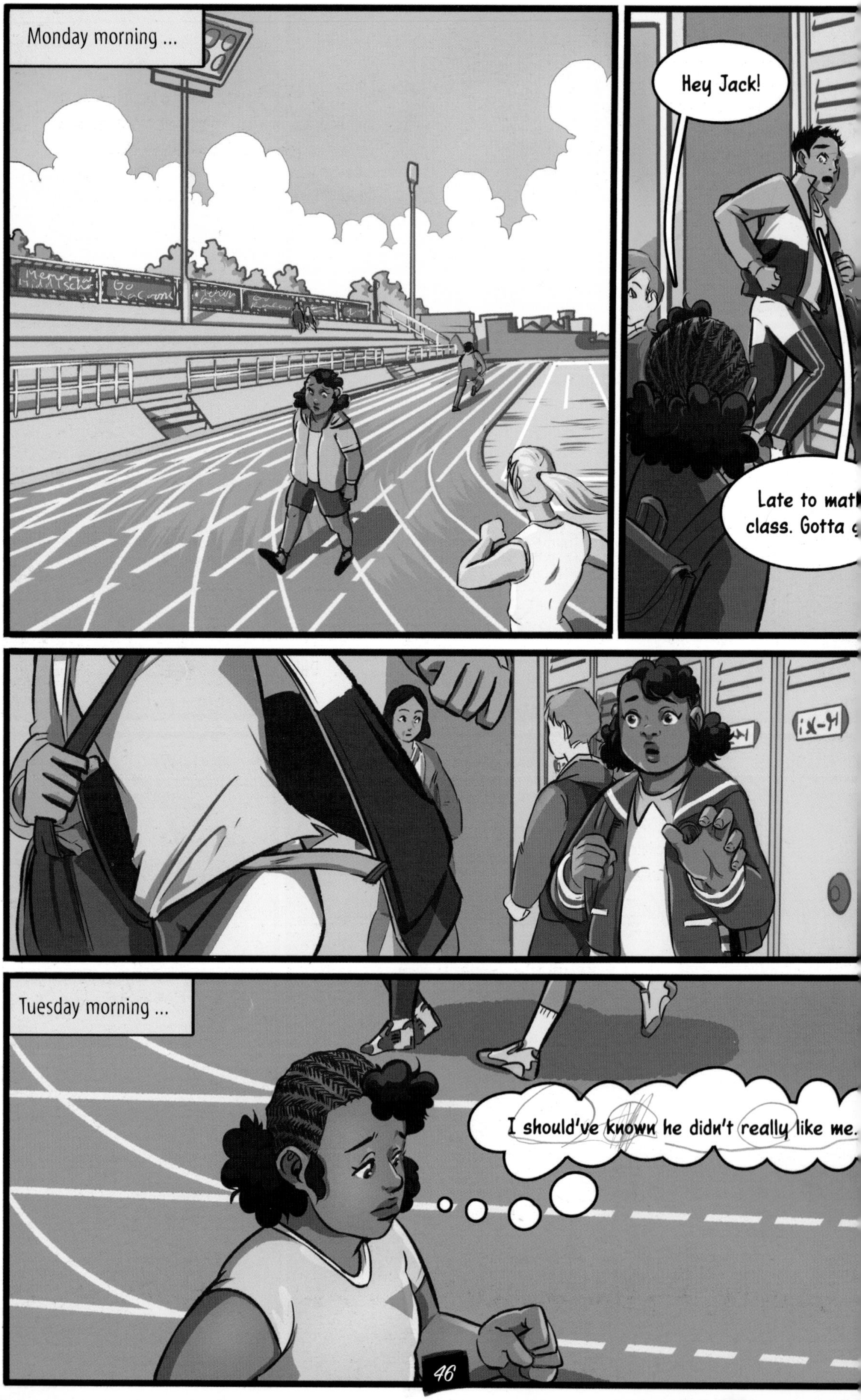
Monday morning ...
Hey Jack!
Late to mat
class. Gotta
Tuesday morning ...
I should've known he didn't really like me.

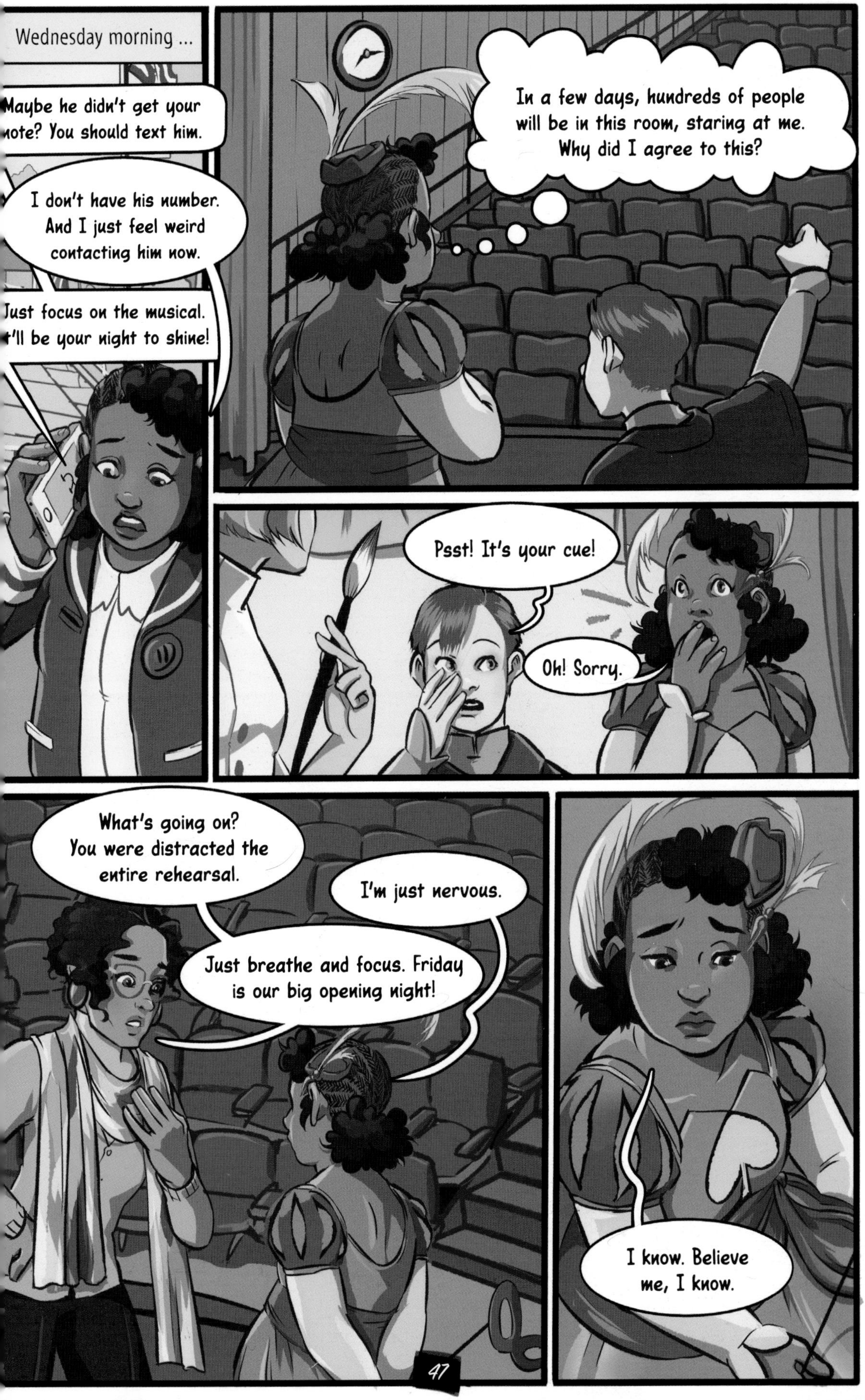
Wednesday morning ...
Maybe he didn't get your note? You should text him.
I don't have his number. And I just feel weird contacting him now.
Just focus on the musical. It'll be your night to shine!
In a few days, hundreds of people will be in this room, staring at me. Why did I agree to this?
Psst! It's your cue!
Oh! Sorry.
What's going on? You were distracted the entire rehearsal.
I'm just nervous.
Just breathe and focus. Friday is our big opening night!
I know. Believe me, I know.

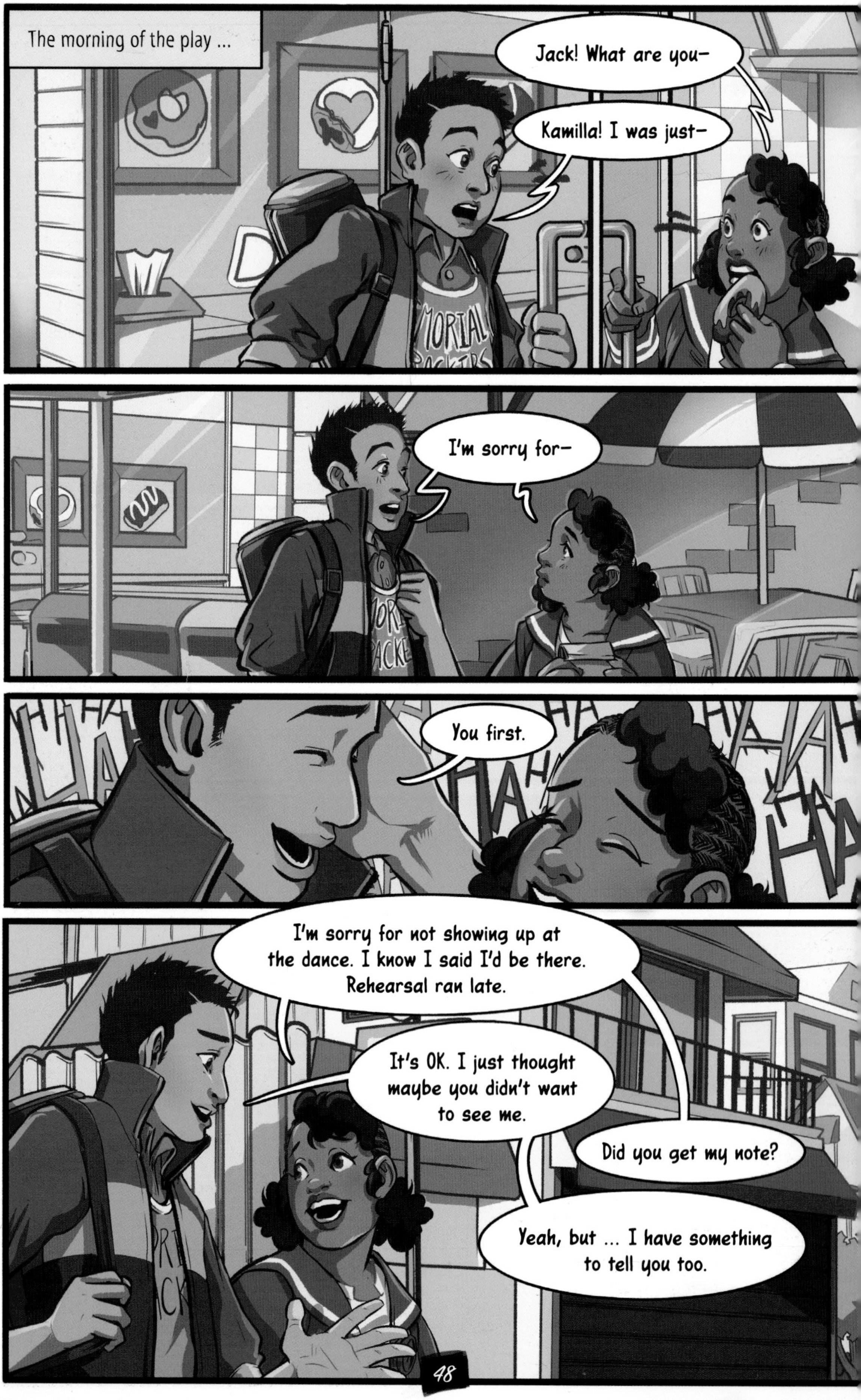
The morning of the play ...
Jack! What are you–
Kamilla! I was just–
I'm sorry for–
HA HA HA
You first.
I'm sorry for not showing up at the dance. I know I said I'd be there. Rehearsal ran late.
It's OK. I just thought maybe you didn't want to see me.
Did you get my note?
Yeah, but ... I have something to tell you too.

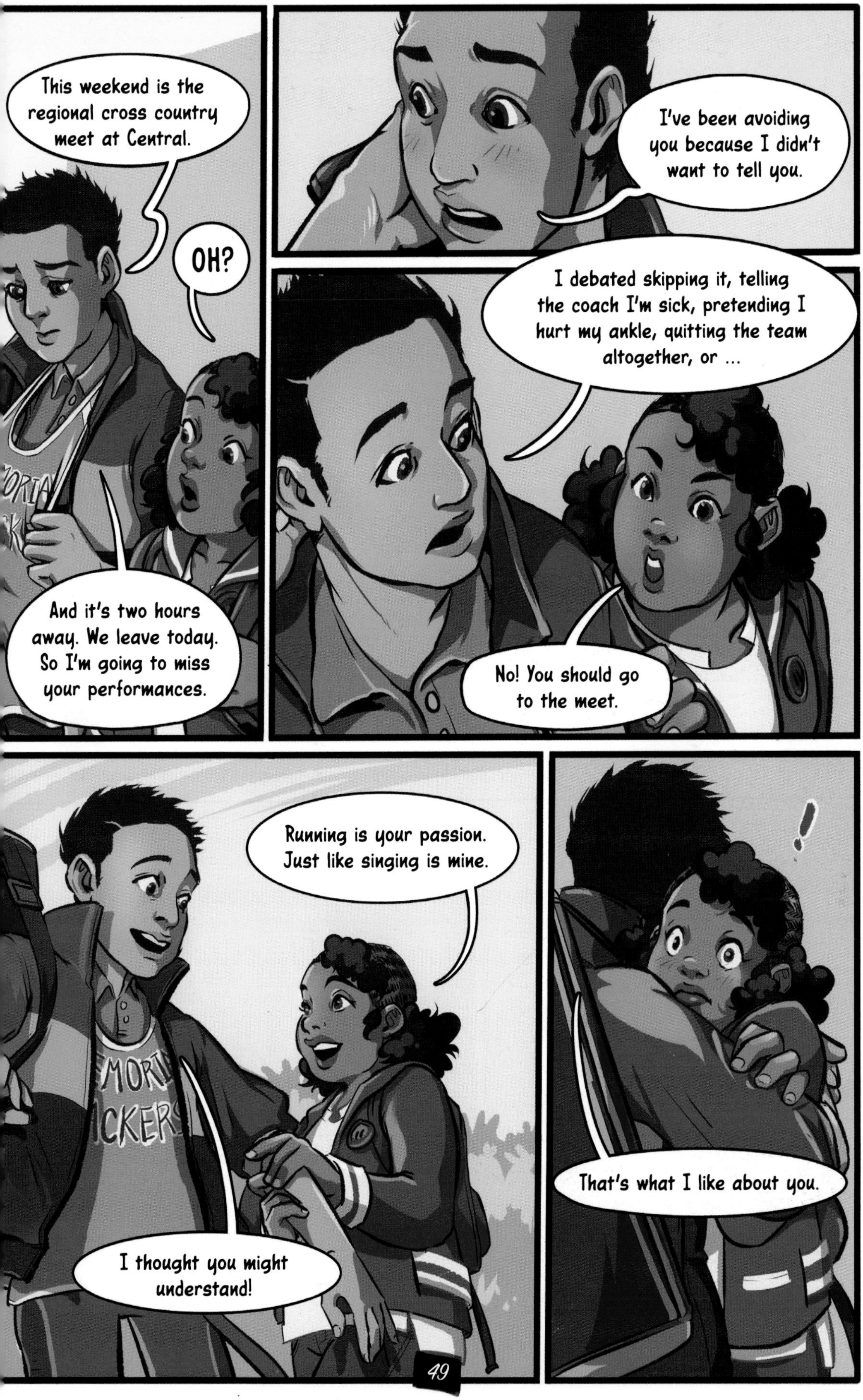
This weekend is the regional cross country meet at Central.
OH?
And it's two hours away. We leave today. So I'm going to miss your performances.
I've been avoiding you because I didn't want to tell you.
I debated skipping it, telling the coach I'm sick, pretending I hurt my ankle, quitting the team altogether, or ...
No! You should go to the meet.
Running is your passion. Just like singing is mine.
I thought you might understand!
!
That's what I like about you.

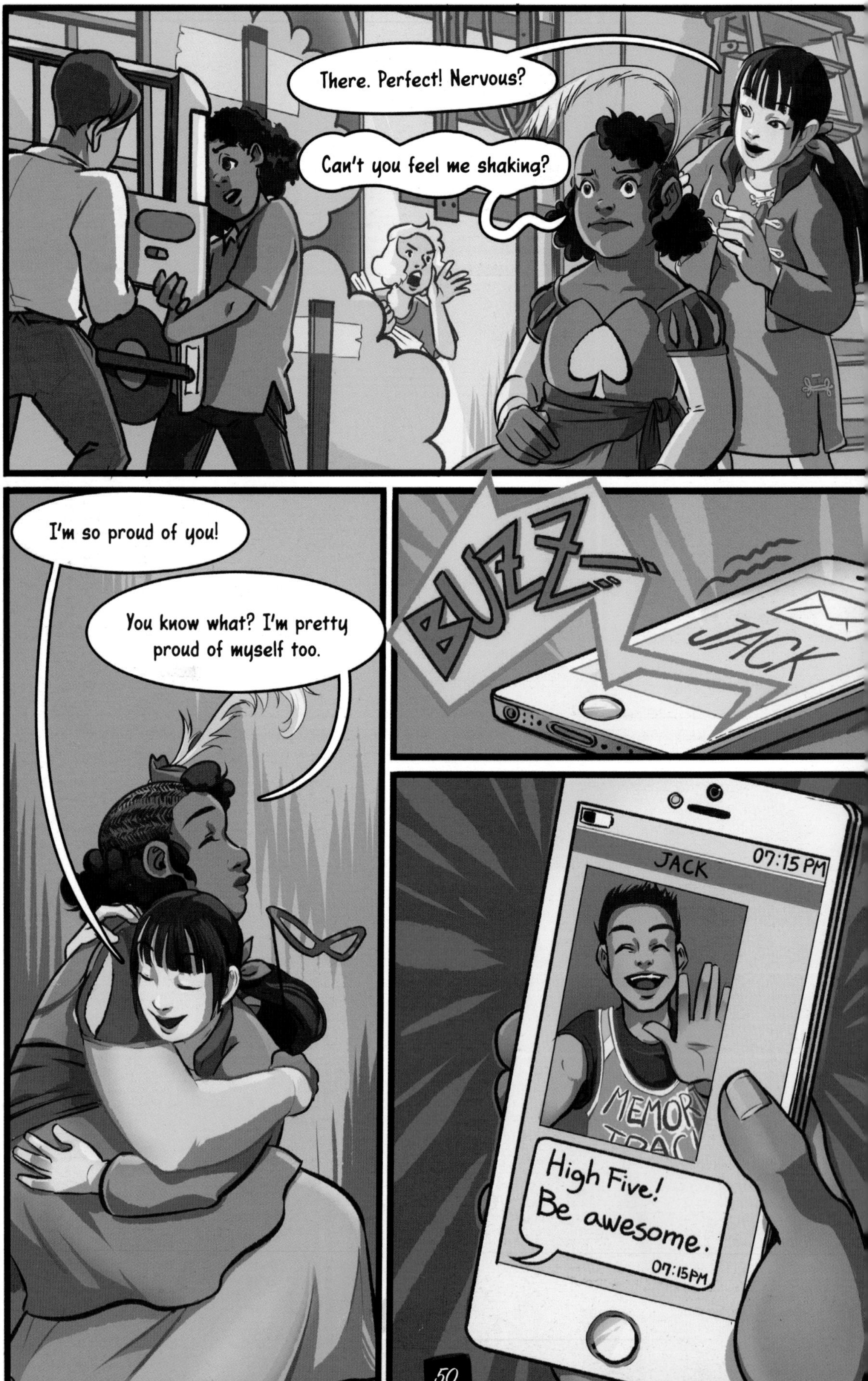
There. Perfect! Nervous?
Can't you feel me shaking?
I'm so proud of you!
You know what? I'm pretty proud of myself too.
BUZZ—
JACK
JACK
07:15 PM
High Five! Be awesome.
07:15PM

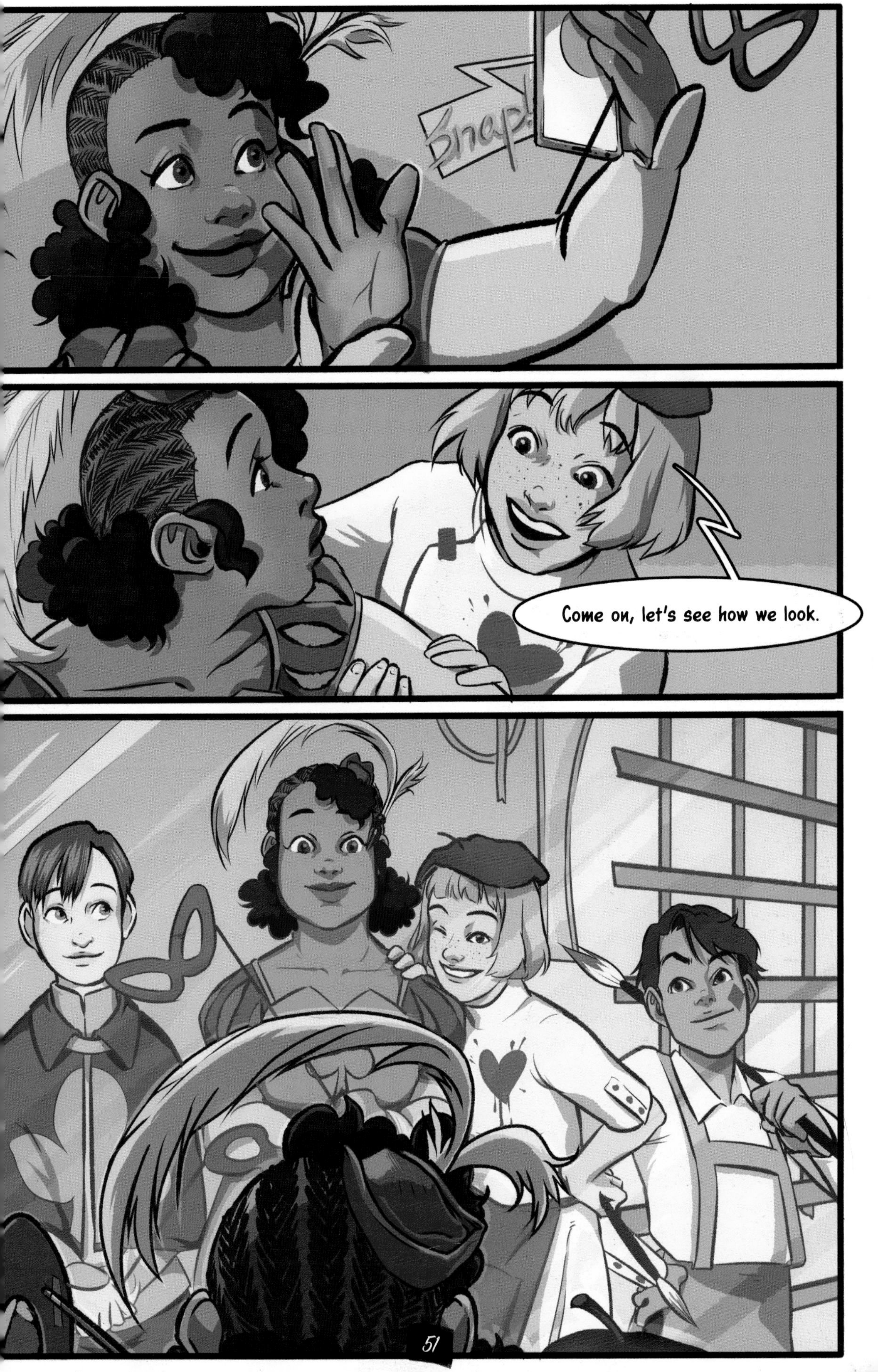
Snap!
Come on, let's see how we look.

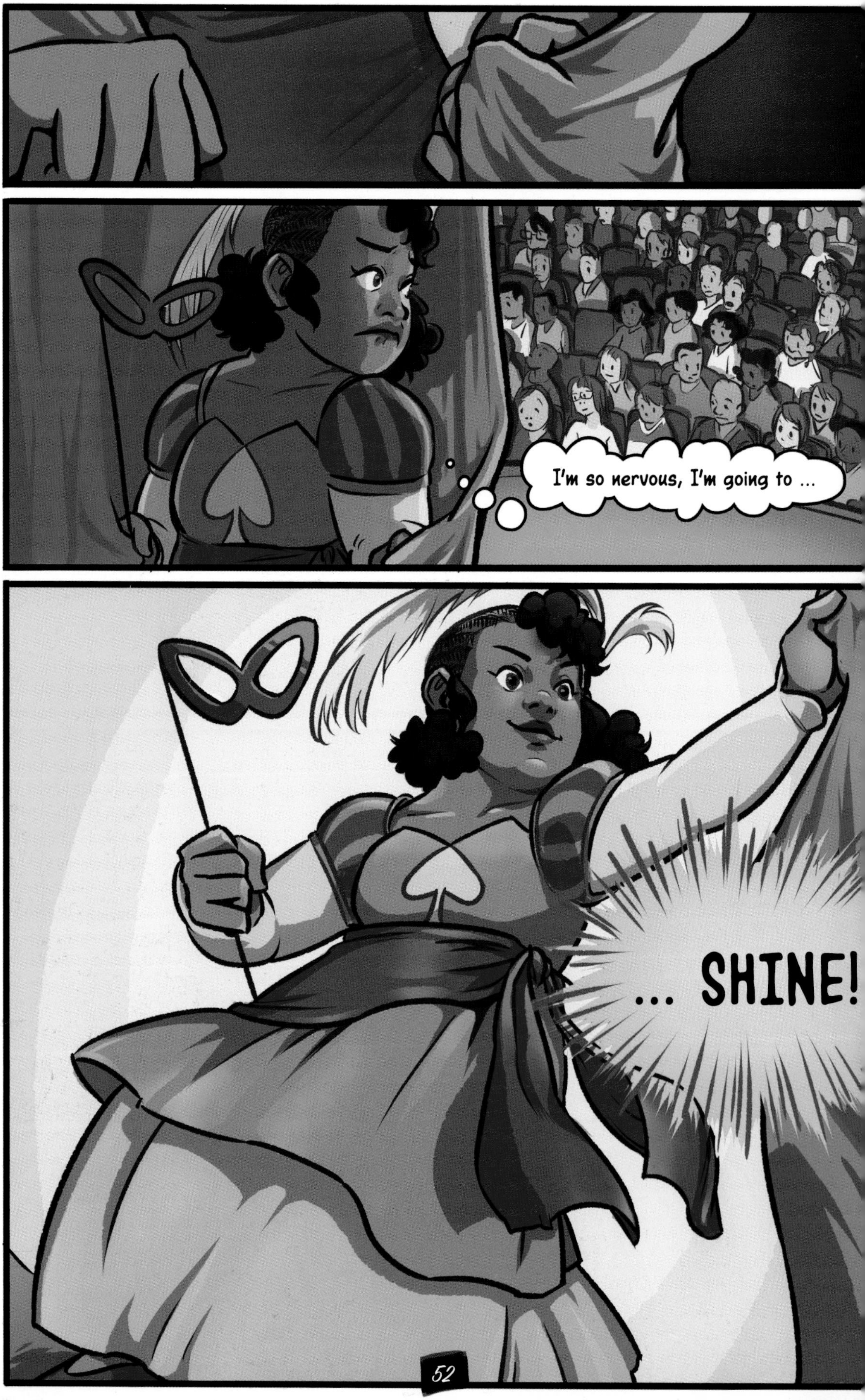

I'm so nervous, I'm going to ...
... SHINE!

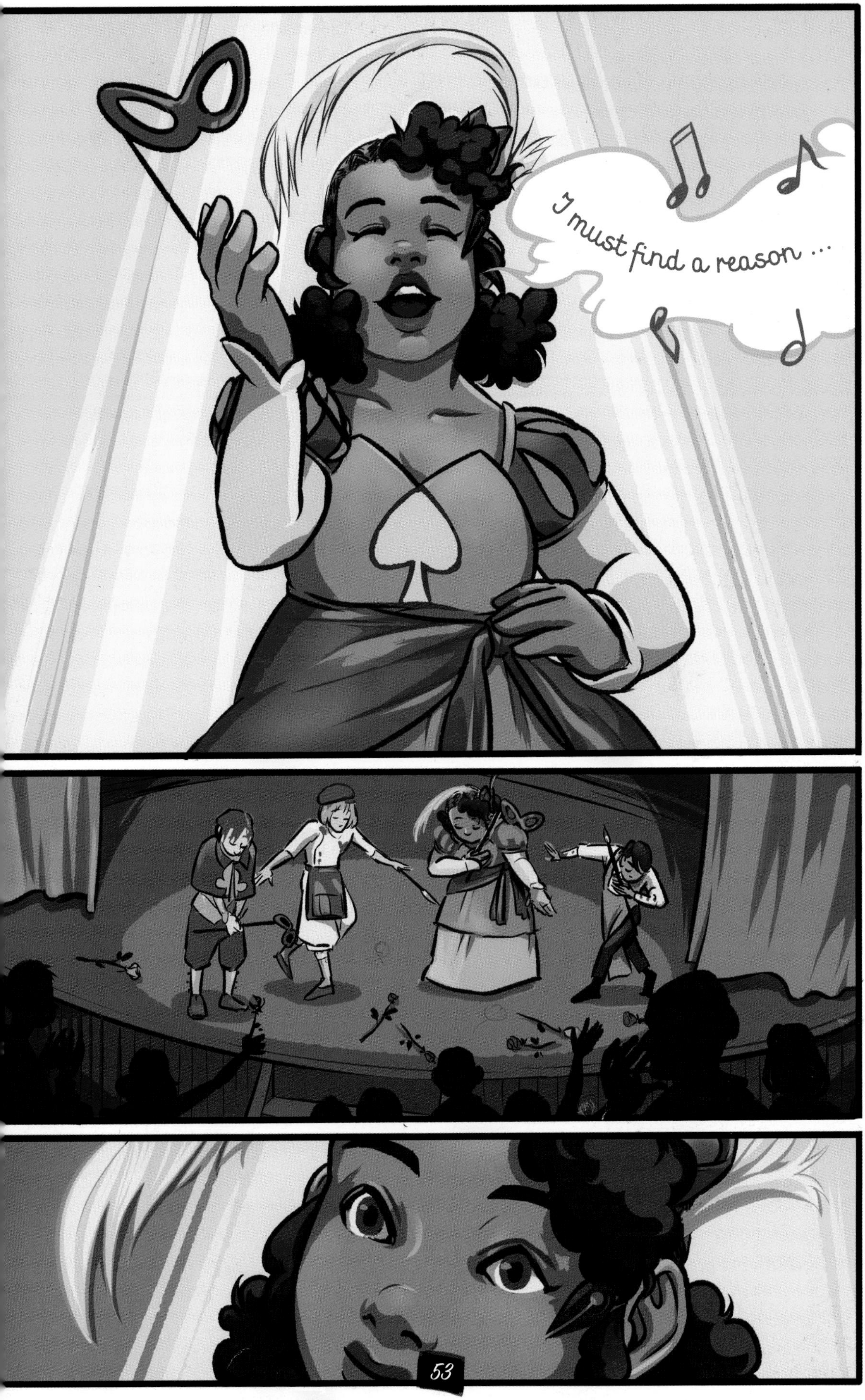
I must find a reason ...

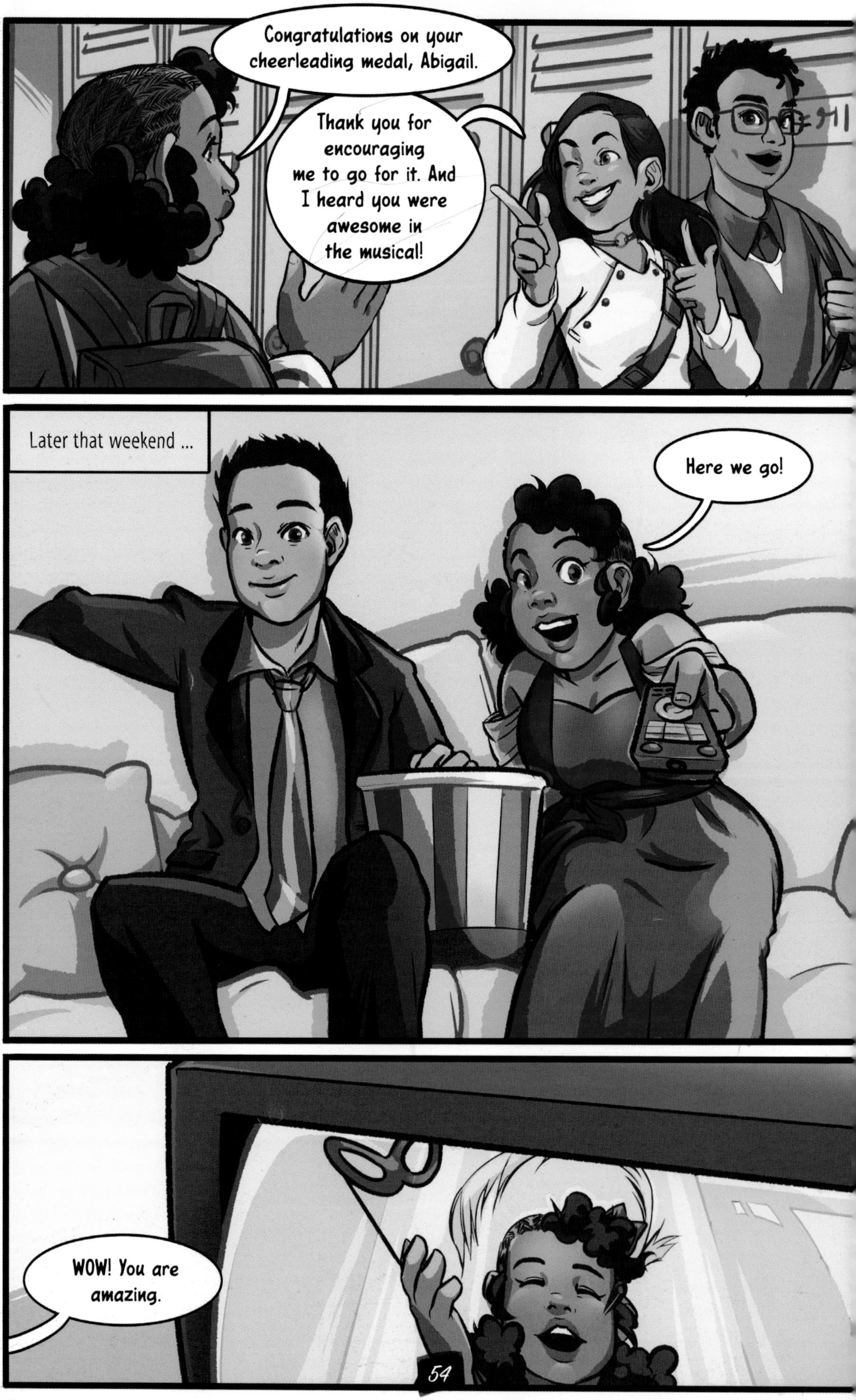
Congratulations on your cheerleading medal, Abigail.
Thank you for encouraging me to go for it. And I heard you were awesome in the musical!
Later that weekend ...
Here we go!
WOW! You are amazing.

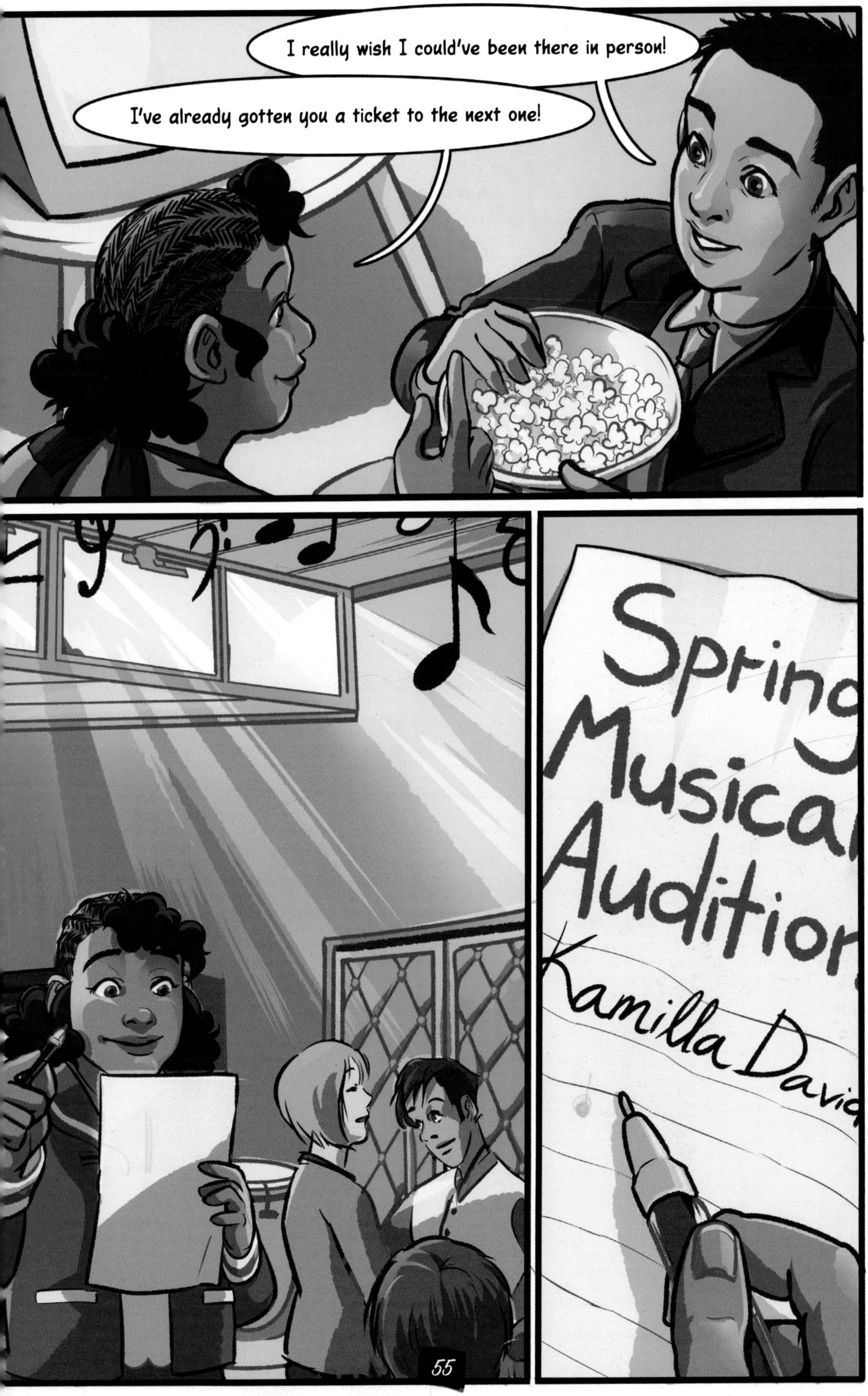
I really wish I could've been there in person!
I've already gotten you a ticket to the next one!
Sprin
Musica
Audition
Kamilla Davi

# Drama Club!

The highlight of Drama Club's year was *KATS*, an original musical by our own Ms. Gray. The club organized everything from publicity and props to costumes and cast party.

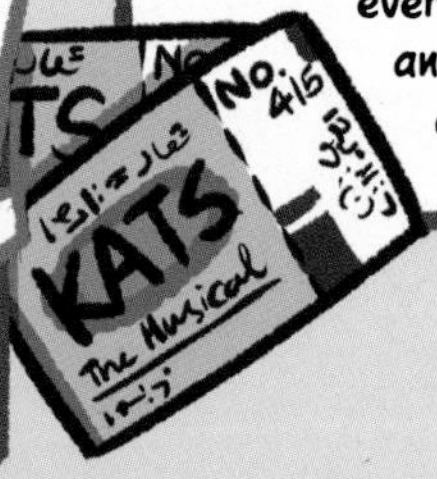

KATS
The Musical
No. 416


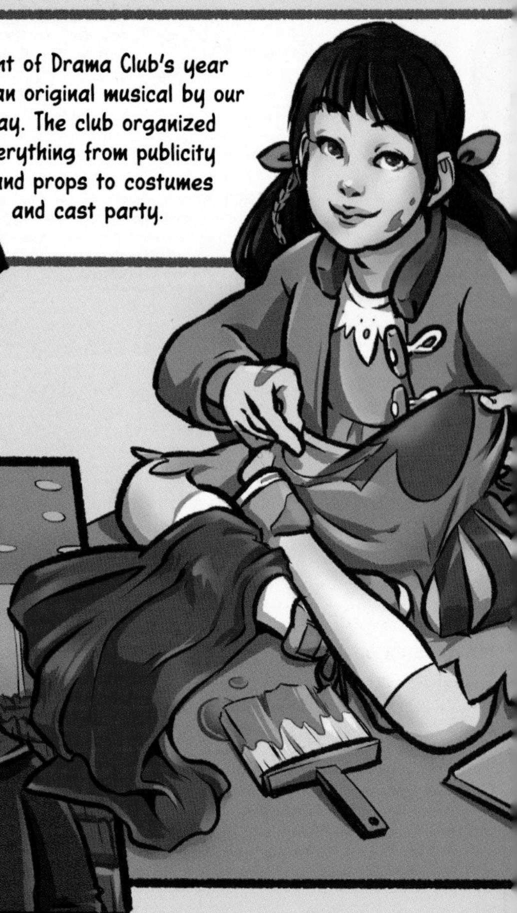

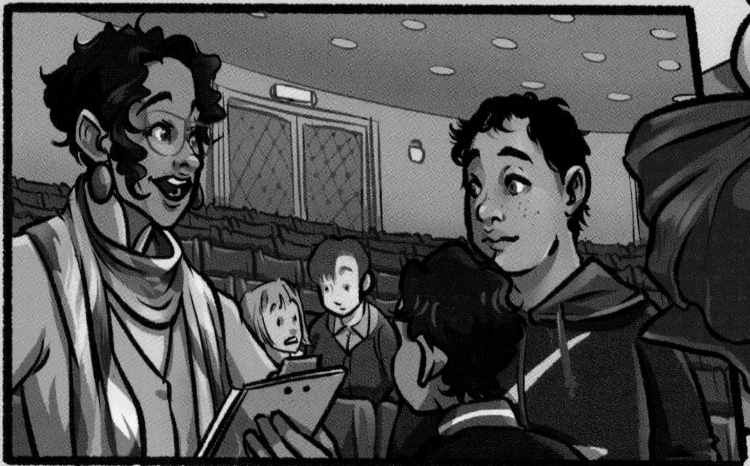

Choir teacher Ms. Gray (left) directs members of the chorus.

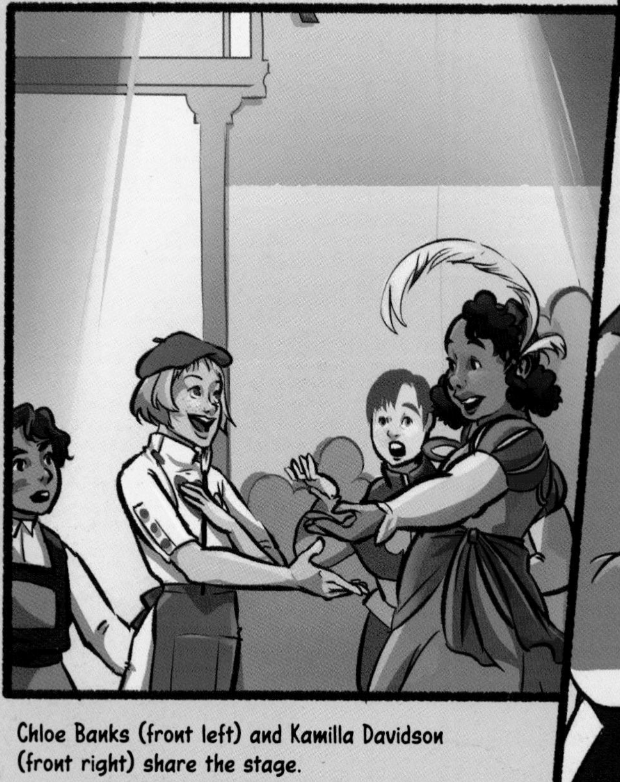

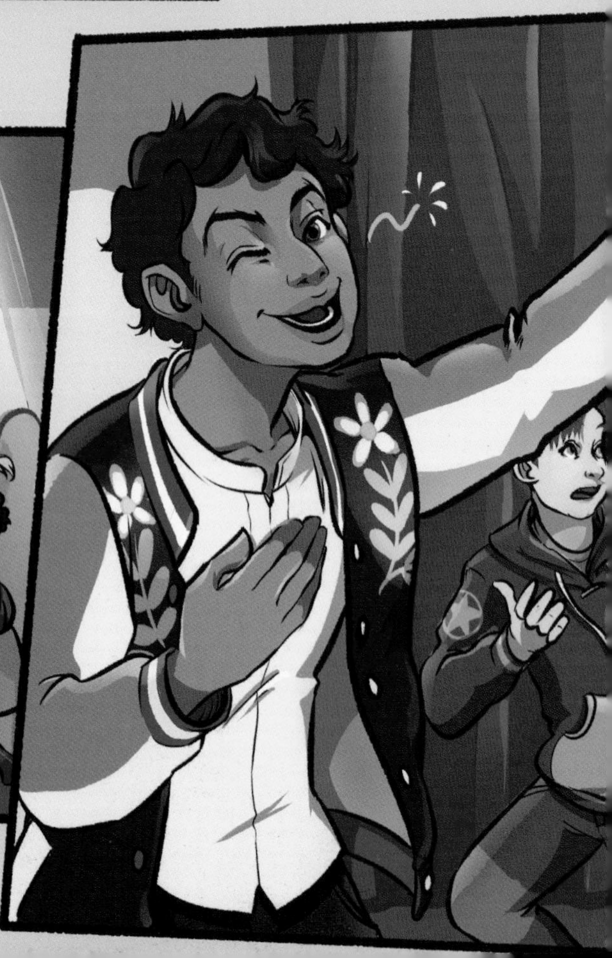

Chloe Banks (front left) and Kamilla Davidson (front right) share the stage.

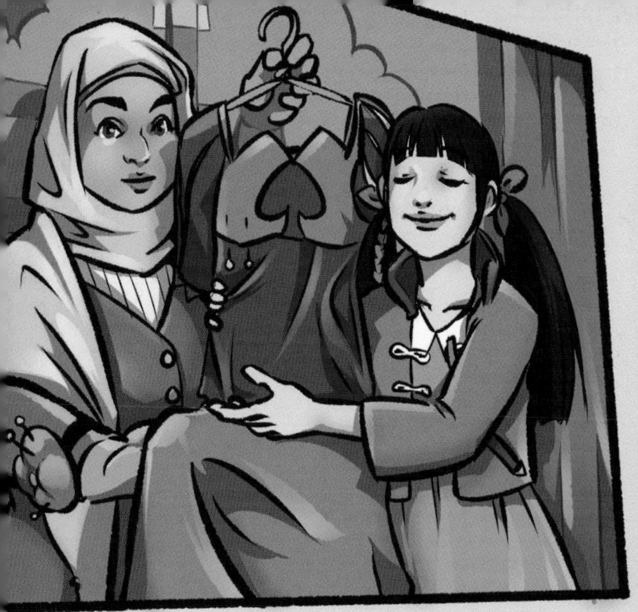

(Above, from left to right) Dalia Darb and Jasmine Yu prepare costumes on opening night of the show. (Right, top to bottom) Tom Rawson, Franny Luca, and Samir Patel work on the set.

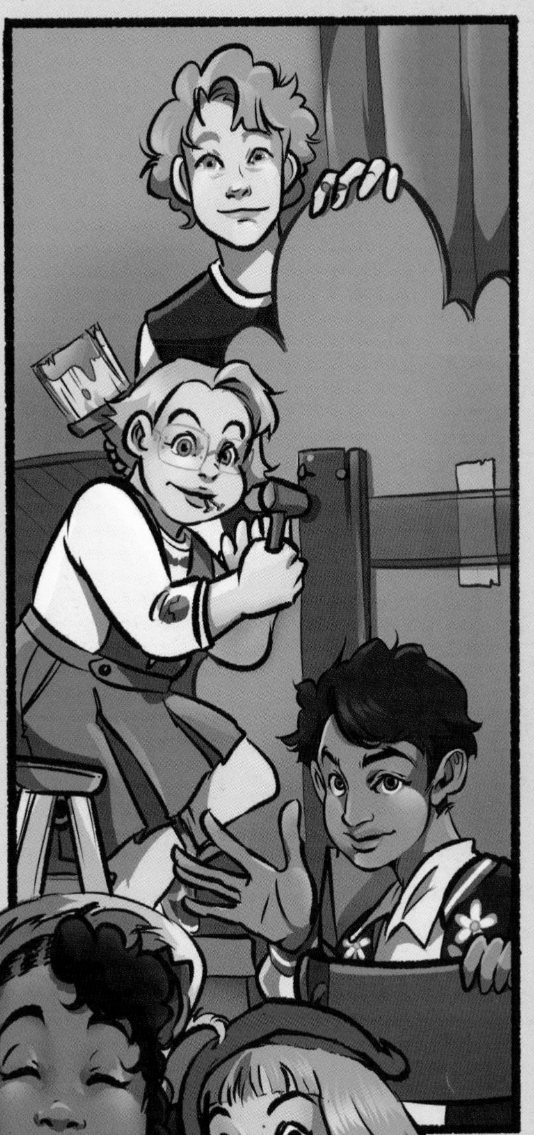

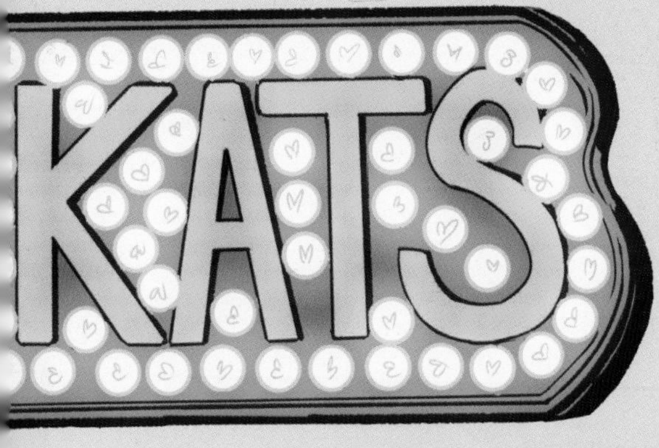
KATS

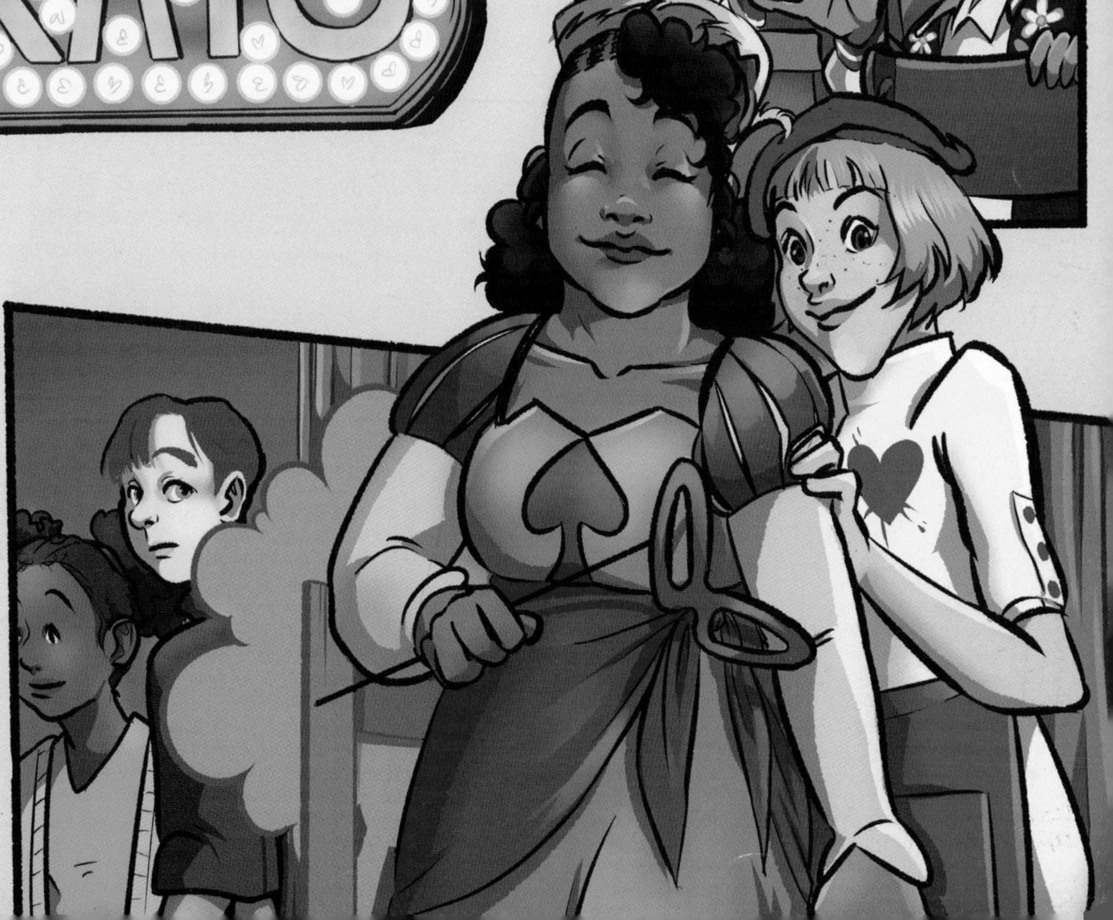

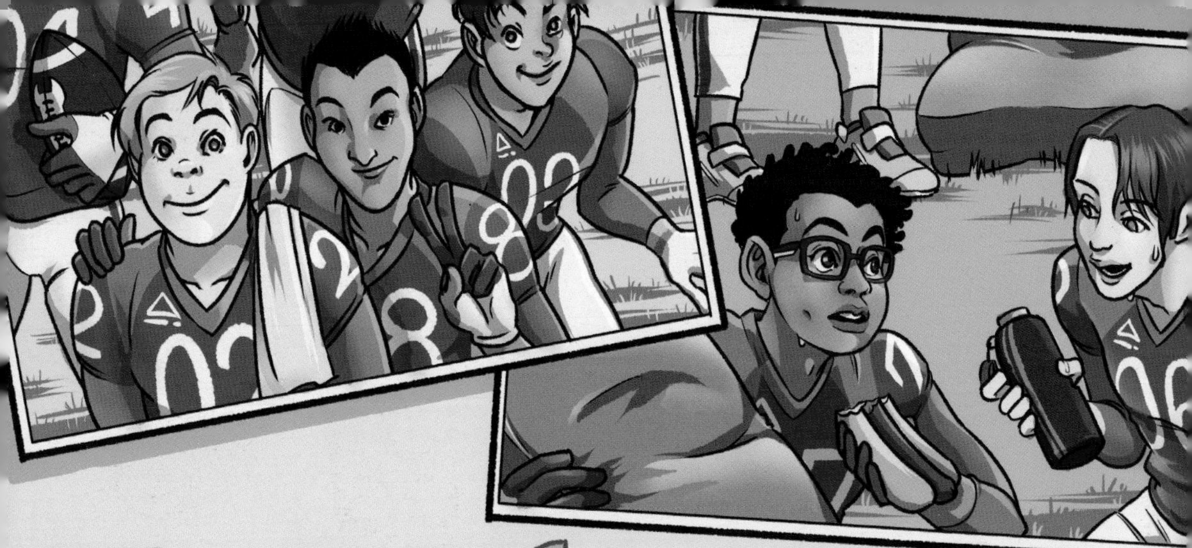

Starting player Noah Patrick enjoys a hot dog at the Homecoming Hot Dog Feed.

# Football

## Go Raccoons!

1 The Raccoon footba
team finished the
season with a winn
record: 8-2.

2 In the biggest gam
of the season, the
Raccoons beat the
biggest rival, the
Madison Bulldogs, 1

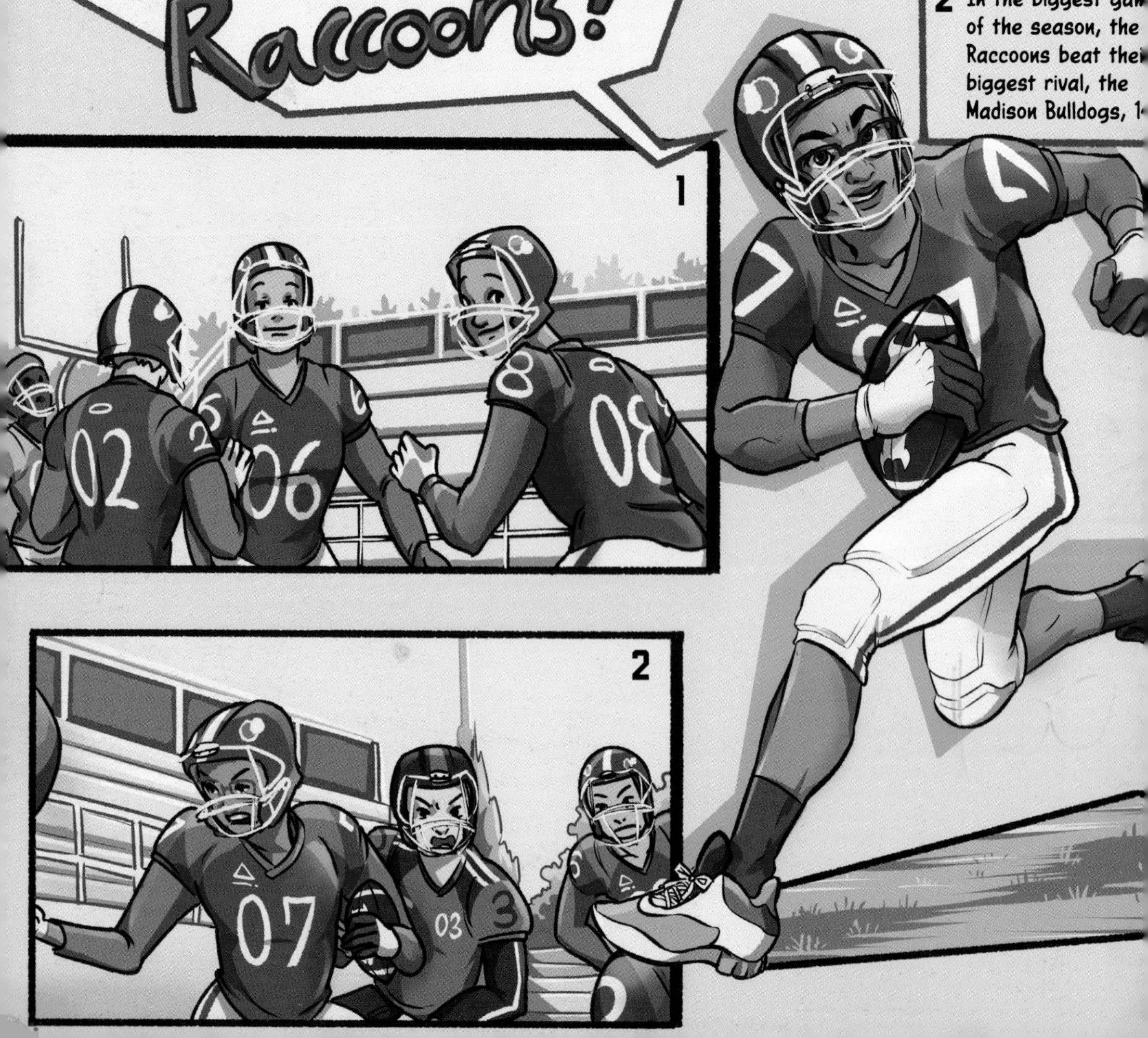
1
2

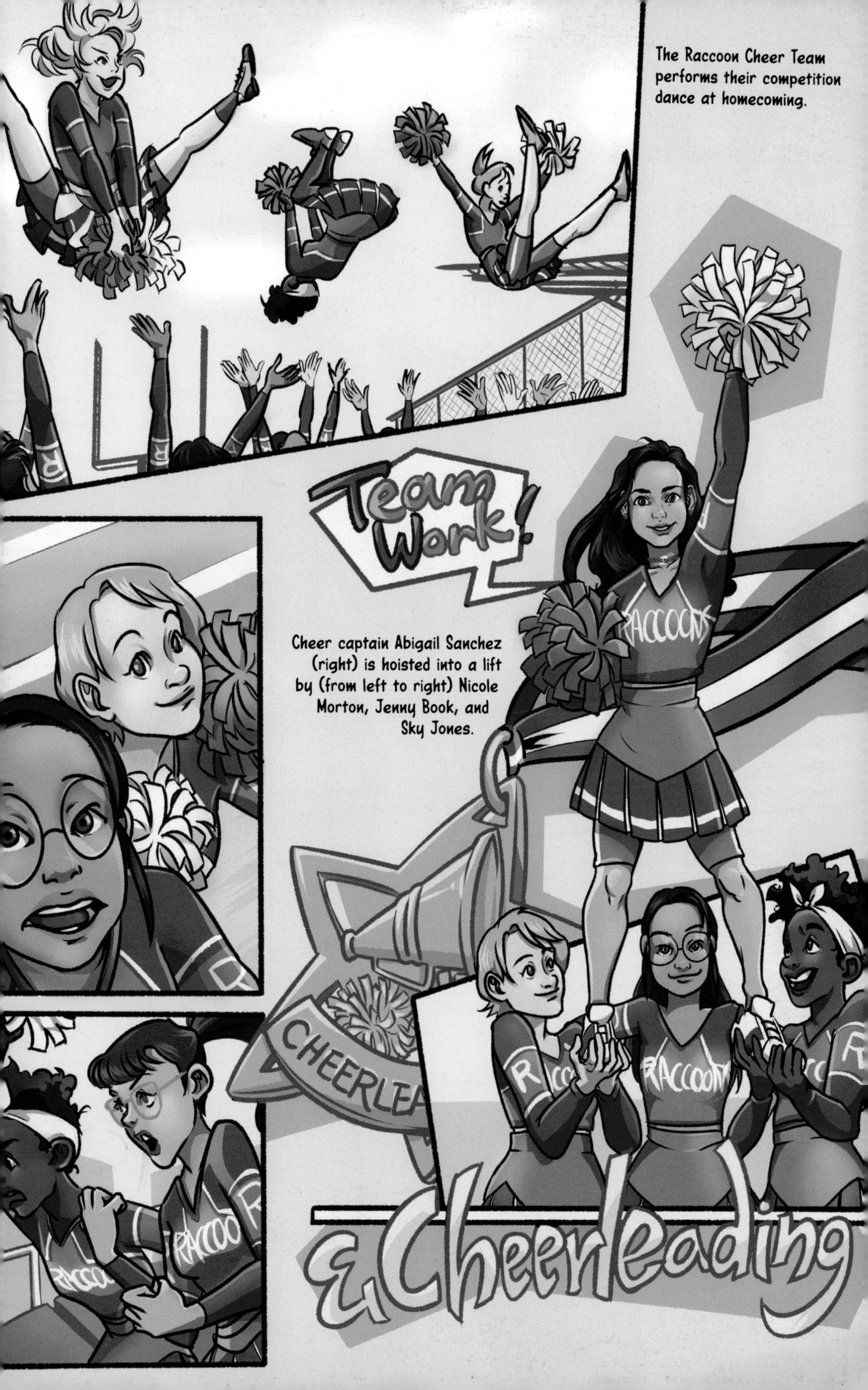
Team Work!
CHEERLEA
RACCOONS
& Cheerleading

The Raccoon Cheer Team performs their competition dance at homecoming.

Cheer captain Abigail Sanchez (right) is hoisted into a lift by (from left to right) Nicole Morton, Jenny Book, and Sky Jones.

*There is no wrong way to have a body.* –GLENN MARLA

# CONFIDENC

GIRLS START EXPRESSING CONCERN ABOUT THEIR BODY AND WEIGHT AS EARLY AS AGE SIX.

**77%** **of girls say they want to look their bes rather than follow someone else's definition o "BEAUTIFUL**

OF GIRLS WHO REA MAGAZINES, **47%** SAY TH IMAGES MAKE THEM WAN TO LOSE WEIGHT. **69%** SA THE IMAGES INFLUENC WHAT THEY CONSIDE AN IDEAL BODY SHAP

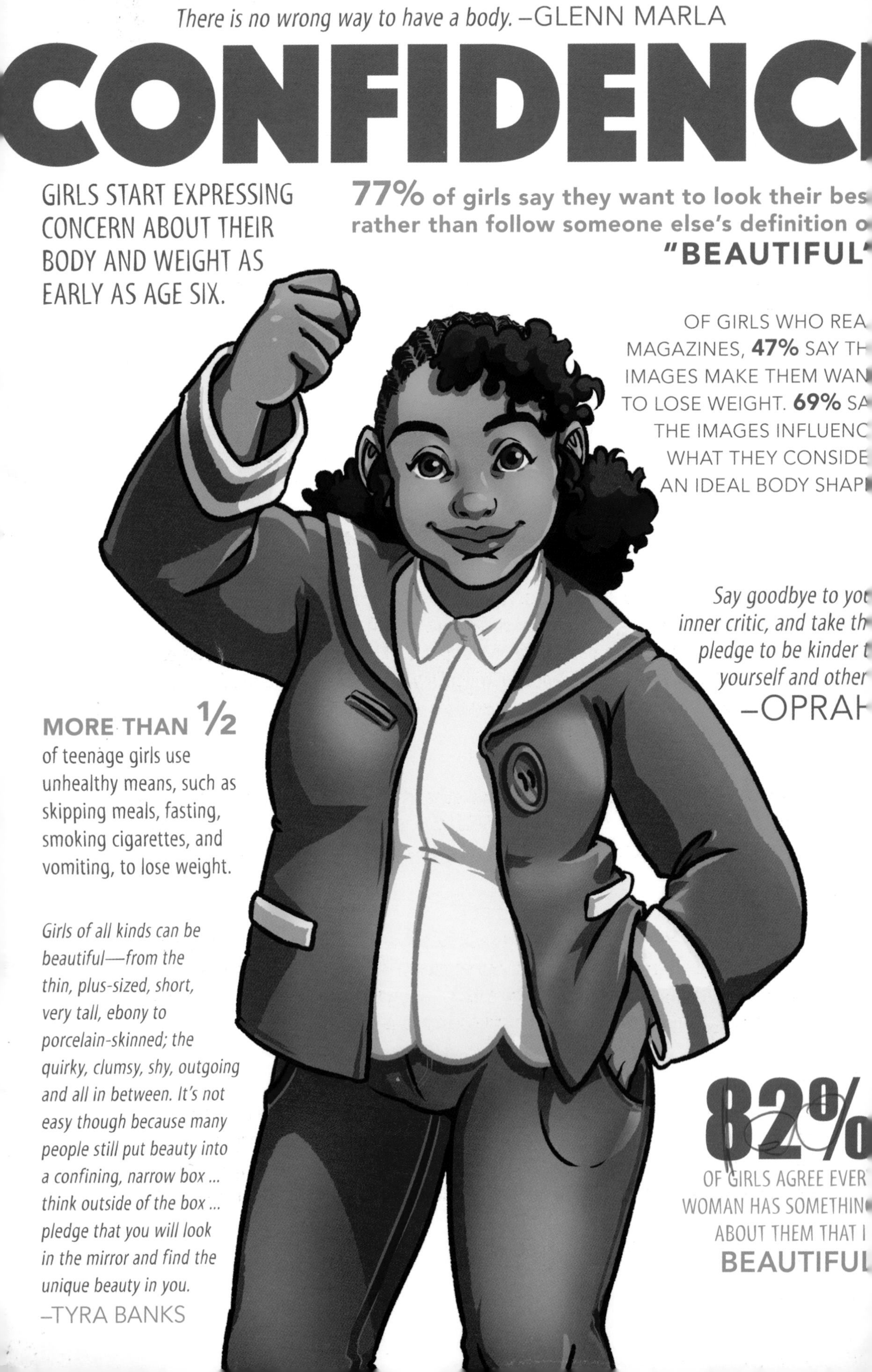

*Say goodbye to yo inner critic, and take th pledge to be kinder t yourself and other*
–OPRAH

**MORE THAN ½**
of teenage girls use unhealthy means, such as skipping meals, fasting, smoking cigarettes, and vomiting, to lose weight.

*Girls of all kinds can be beautiful—from the thin, plus-sized, short, very tall, ebony to porcelain-skinned; the quirky, clumsy, shy, outgoing and all in between. It's not easy though because many people still put beauty into a confining, narrow box ... think outside of the box ... pledge that you will look in the mirror and find the unique beauty in you.*
–TYRA BANKS

**82%**
OF GIRLS AGREE EVER WOMAN HAS SOMETHIN ABOUT THEM THAT I **BEAUTIFUL**

# KAMILLA INTERVIEWS
## ⟫⟫⟫ ⟫ DR. CHUA ⟪ ⟪⟪⟪⟪

**KAMILLA:** Hi Dr. Chua! Thank you so much for letting me interview you for my school project. I really appreciate it.

**DR. CHUA:** It's my pleasure, Kamilla. I'm more than happy to help. It's important to me that people, especially young people, are properly informed to have a positive body image.

**K:** That's where I'd like to start. What's the difference between self-esteem and body image? They seem pretty similar from where I'm sitting.

**DC:** You're absolutely right! The two are very similar. Imagine that your self-esteem is a pie. The pie represents everything you value or do not value about yourself. Body image is only a piece of that pie. Having a positive or negative body image can influence your self-esteem.

**K:** That's interesting you chose pie as an example. I read online that if I eat apple pie as a meal for a week, I'll lose ten pounds!

**DC:** That sounds like a fad diet, Kamilla. Fad diets are dangerous, and they rarely ever work. They promise a lot of weight loss in a short amount of time, even though it's generally unhealthy to lose more than one to two pounds per week. Plus, fad diets cut out major food groups that you need for balanced nutrition. If you only eat pie, you could be low on vitamin B-12, which leads to muscle weakness.

**K:** OK, so no pie diets. What do you recommend then?

**DC:** First, I would recommend changing your motivation. Instead of thinking, "I want to lose weight," try, "I want to become healthier." Second, focus on having a balanced, nutritious diet. Third, exercise. These things will help you to create healthy, lifelong habits.

**K:** But how much exercise do young people need?

**DC:** Well, children and teenagers should do aerobic activity, such as walking or jogging, for sixty minutes every day. They should also do muscle-strengthening exercises and bone-strengthening exercises at least three days a week. Push-ups could count as muscle strengthening, and jump rope is a good exercise for bone strengthening.

**K:** And that will help people lose weight?

**DC:** It's not about weight, Kamilla. Weighing less does not necessarily mean that you are healthy. Just as weighing less does not automatically give you a healthy body image. Positive body image starts with a positive attitude. The most important thing you can do is develop a happy, healthy relationship with your body—no matter what kind of shape it is.

**K:** That is great advice, Dr. C! Thanks again!

# GLOSSARY

**ALTERNATE**—a person named to take the place of another when necessary

**AUDITION**—a short performance by an actor, singer, musician, or dancer to see whether he or she is suitable for a part in a play, concert, etc.

**FLUCTUATIONS**—back-and-forth or up-and-down changes

**GURU**—a person with knowledge and expertise

**OVEREXERT**—to overwork or overdo something

**SABOTAGE**—to damage or hurt something or someone on purpose

# WHAT DO YOU THINK?

1. How does Kamilla's body language change from the beginning of the story to the end of the story?

2. Based on Tyler's facial expressions on page 20, what do you think he thinks of Kamilla's singing?

3. Reread pages 30–32. What happened to Abigail at the State Cheer Competition? Write a story about her experience there.

4. Throughout the book, did anyone other than Kamilla ever say anything negative about Kamilla's body, or was it all in Kamilla's thoughts? Name three things Kamilla could do to be more positive.

5. Imagine Kamilla's school is putting on another musical. Describe how Kamilla will behave differently this time around.

### CHALLENGE!

Say something nice! Compliment a person on a choice they've made that day. Something as small as a smile can turn someone's day around!

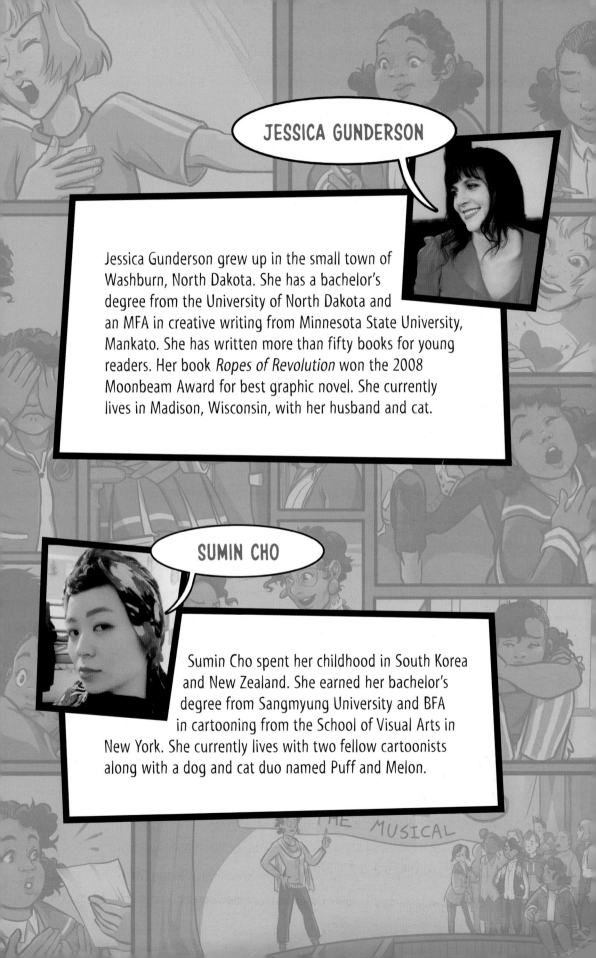

## JESSICA GUNDERSON

Jessica Gunderson grew up in the small town of Washburn, North Dakota. She has a bachelor's degree from the University of North Dakota and an MFA in creative writing from Minnesota State University, Mankato. She has written more than fifty books for young readers. Her book *Ropes of Revolution* won the 2008 Moonbeam Award for best graphic novel. She currently lives in Madison, Wisconsin, with her husband and cat.

## SUMIN CHO

Sumin Cho spent her childhood in South Korea and New Zealand. She earned her bachelor's degree from Sangmyung University and BFA in cartooning from the School of Visual Arts in New York. She currently lives with two fellow cartoonists along with a dog and cat duo named Puff and Melon.

# WANT MORE DRAMA?



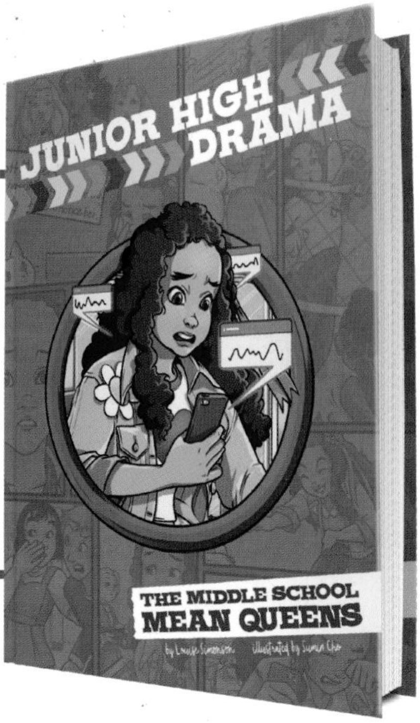
JUNIOR HIGH DRAMA
THE MIDDLE SCHOOL
MEAN QUEENS

Lilly wants to hang out with the popular girls, so she's excited when a birthday party invitation arrives from queen bee Tania. What Lilly doesn't realize is that Tania plans to use Lilly to get to her cute older brother, Hank. When Tania's plan fails, she blames Lilly, making her life a nightmare. Will Lilly survive the mean queens of middle school?

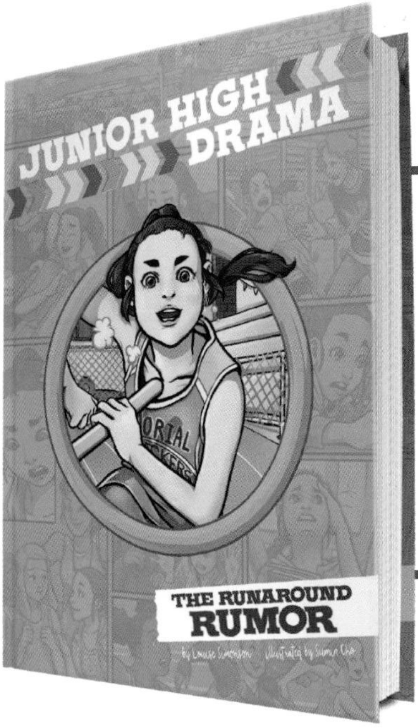
JUNIOR HIGH DRAMA
THE RUNAROUND
RUMOR

Allie's world is turned upside down when she's diagnosed with diabetes. Her overprotective parents are driving her crazy, and she's desperate to keep her condition a secret from her friends. But her secretive ways are awfully suspicious and soon the rumors are flying. Is Allie's reputation ruined for good?

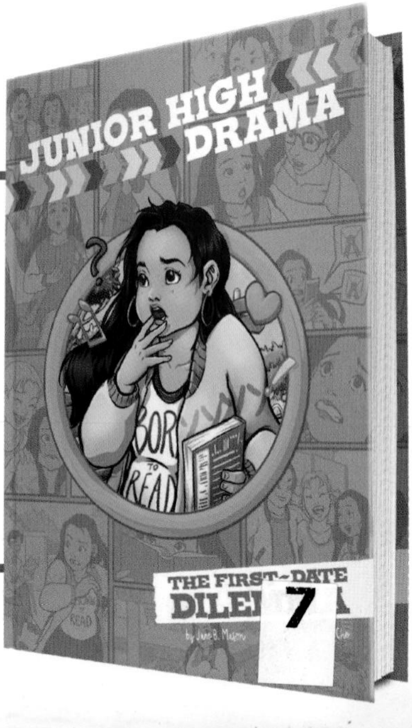
JUNIOR HIGH DRAMA
THE FIRST-DATE

The eighth graders at Memorial Middle School are obsessing about their first boy-girl party. Lucia is sick of hearing about what to wear and who's going together. If her best friend hadn't insisted, she wouldn't even go to the dumb party. But after she gets to know Adesh, Lucia starts thinking the party might not be too bad ... until she realizes he's interested in another girl.